Tears of the Giraffe

ALEXANDER McCALL SMITH

Level 4

Retold by John Potter
Series Editors: Andy Hopkins and Jocelyn Potter

Pearson Education Limited
Edinburgh Gate, Harlow,
Essex CM20 2JE, England
and Associated Companies throughout the world.

ISBN: 978-1-4058-6777-1

This edition first published by Pearson Education Ltd 2008

1 3 5 7 9 10 8 6 4 2

Text copyright © Pearson Education Ltd 2008
Illustrations by Doreen Lang

Set in 11/14pt Bembo
Printed in China
SWTC/01

Published by Pearson Education Limited in association with
Penguin Books Ltd, both companies being subsidiaries of Pearson PLC

For a complete list of the titles available in the Penguin Readers series please write to your local
Pearson Longman office or to: Penguin Readers Marketing Department, Pearson Education,
Edinburgh Gate, Harlow, Essex CM20 2JE

Contents

Introduction

What could she do for this woman, if the Botswana Police and the American Embassy had tried and failed? But the woman needed help, and if she could not get help from the No. 1 Ladies' Detective Agency, then where could she get it?

Precious Ramotswe, a wise and kind woman with a good sense of humour, is the first female private detective in Botswana. Her agency, The No. 1 Ladies' Detective Agency, has helped many people with their problems – stolen cars, missing relatives and lying husbands and wives.

Mma* Ramotswe has a traditional love of her country and her family. Her size is traditional too – she is a large lady. Her favourite drink is red bush tea, which she always drinks with her clients. She solves their problems with hard work, intelligence and an ability to know when people are telling the truth.

Her office is in a small building in Gaborone, the capital of Botswana. It contains two desks, three chairs, an old typewriter and an old teapot which her secretary, Mma Makutsi, uses to make the bush tea. Sometimes there are also chickens.

Mma Ramotswe drives a little white van, which often breaks down. That is how she met her good friend Mr JLB Matekoni, the best mechanic in Botswana. After a bad marriage to a musician, Mma Ramotswe is single again, and Mr JLB Matekoni has just asked her to marry him.

In *Tears of the Giraffe*, Mma Ramotswe accepts the difficult – and possibly dangerous – case of a missing child. Her clever secretary, Mma Makutsi, finds that she has to do more than

---

* Mma: *Mrs* or *Madam* in Setswana, the language spoken by most people in Botswana

make bush tea. And Mr JLB Matekoni suddenly has to take care of more than broken vans.

Alexander McCall Smith, like his character Mma Ramotswe, has had an interesting life. He was born in Zimbabwe, and went to school there and in Scotland. He taught law at a university in Scotland, and returned to Africa to start a new law school at the University of Botswana. He now lives in Edinburgh, Scotland.

He has written more than sixty books, including books about law, books of short stories, mystery stories and children's books. His fiction is full of humour and wonderful characters.

But his most popular books are the ones about Mma Ramotswe. These books have been translated into thirty-nine languages and have sold over fourteen million copies around the world. The first of these books, *The No. 1 Ladies' Detective Agency*, tells readers how Mma Ramotswe began the agency and how she solved her first cases. It is also a Penguin Reader. There are now eight books about Mma Ramotswe and her friends.

These stories have made people everywhere interested in her beautiful country, Botswana. It is a small country, with fewer than two million people. Most of it is covered by the Kalahari Desert, but it is also home to many different sorts of animals and birds, which visitors come to see.

Like most other African countries, for many years Botswana was controlled by Europeans. Britain governed Botswana from 1885 until 1966, when Botswana became independent.

Botswana has been called an African success story. The schools are good and the economy is growing. Gaborone, Mma Ramotswe's home, is the fastest-growing city in Africa. But there are problems, too. Many people in the country suffer from AIDS*. There is more crime than before. At the same

* AIDS: a very serious disease that often causes death

time, traditional African ways of life are disappearing, and new buildings and lifestyles are taking their place.

Mma Ramotswe and her friend Mr JLB Matekoni are proud of modern Botswana, but they miss the old ways and try to live by traditional values.

The main characters take their duty of responsibility for other people seriously. They learn that they have to keep their promises, although it is not always easy to do that. They have to make difficult decisions that affect the lives of other people. McCall Smith shows that the world would be a better place if we all took more responsibility for the people around us.

Africa is not just the background of *Tears of the Giraffe*. It is an important part of the story. It is easy to share McCall Smith's love of Africa when we read his descriptions of the land, its people and its animals. For readers who have never been to Africa, these descriptions are some of the most wonderful parts of the book.

Each of the main characters in *Tears of a Giraffe* tells a piece of the story from his or her own point of view. This makes the story interesting and allows us to know the characters well – the bad ones as well as the good ones.

When you finish reading *Tears of a Giraffe*, you will probably want to read more. If you have already read *The No. 1 Ladies' Detective Agency*, then look for the other books about Mma Ramotswe and her friends.

ZAMBIA

ANGOLA

ZIMBABWE

NAMIBIA

Okavango

Maun

Bulawayo

Francistown

BOTSWANA

KALAHARI
DESERT

Mahalapye

Mochudi

Molepole

GABORONE

Lobatse

SOUTH AFRICA

0 ⊢—— 100 km

AFRICA

BOTSWANA

Chapter 1   Mr JLB Matekoni's House

Mr JLB Matekoni was the owner of Tlokweng Road Speedy Motors, a garage in Gaborone, the capital of Botswana. He had asked Precious Ramotswe, the only lady private detective in Gaborone, to marry him and, to his great surprise, she had agreed.

It was the second time Mr JLB Matekoni had asked her. Mma* Ramotswe had refused the first time. Probably she would never marry again, he had thought. Her first marriage, to a musician named Note Mokoti, had been a disaster. She was an independent woman now, with her own business, the No.† 1 Ladies' Detective Agency. She lived in a comfortable house in Zebra Drive. Men could be difficult to manage, Mr JLB Matekoni thought, so why would she want to marry?

But one evening, after he had fixed her little white van, Mma Ramotswe had said yes. She had given her answer in such a simple, kind way that Mr JLB Matekoni was sure she was one of the very best women in Botswana. He returned home that evening and thought, 'I am over forty years old. Until now I have not been able to find a wife. I am so fortunate that I must be dreaming.'

But it was true. The next morning he knew that it had really happened. Unless she had changed her mind during the night, he was engaged to be married.

He looked at his watch. It was six o'clock, and the first light of the day was on the tree outside his bedroom window. It would be best to wait an hour or more before he telephoned Mma Ramotswe. It would give her time to get up and make her morning cup of tea.

---

* Mma: *Mrs* or *Madam* in Setswana, the language spoken by most people in Botswana
† No. : short for *number*

He telephoned shortly before seven. Mma Ramotswe asked politely whether he had slept well.

'I slept very well,' said Mr JLB Matekoni. 'I dreamed all night about a clever and beautiful woman who has agreed to marry me.'

He paused. If she had changed her mind, then this was the time that she might tell him.

Mma Ramotswe laughed. 'I never remember my dreams. But if I did, I am sure that I would remember dreaming about that excellent mechanic, my future husband.'

Mr JLB Matekoni smiled. She had not changed her mind.

'Today we must go to the President Hotel for lunch,' he said, 'We shall celebrate this important matter.'

Mma Ramotswe agreed. She said she would be ready at twelve o'clock. Afterwards, perhaps he would allow her to visit his house so she could see what it was like. There were two houses now, and they would have to choose one. Her house on Zebra Drive had many good qualities, but it was rather close to the centre of town. His house was near the old airport. It had a large garden and was quiet, but it was not far from the prison.

♦

After their celebration lunch in the President Hotel, they drove off in Mr JLB Matekoni's pick-up truck to see his house.

'It is not a very tidy house,' said Mr JLB Matekoni. 'I have a maid but she makes it worse, I think. And some rooms in this house have engine parts in them.'

Mma Ramotswe said nothing. Now she knew why Mr JLB Matekoni had never invited her to the house before.

They arrived and Mma Ramotswe sat in the pick-up while Mr JLB Matekoni opened the gate. She noted pieces of paper and other rubbish in the garden. If she moved here – if – that would soon change. She would not want people to think that she allowed her garden to look like that.

2

They entered the house and Mma Ramotswe looked around her. They were in the living room. The furniture was old but good, and on the wall there was a painting of a mountain and a small picture of Nelson Mandela.

'This is a very fine room,' said Mma Ramotswe.

Mr JLB Matekoni looked pleased. 'I try to keep this room tidy,' he said. 'It is a special room for important visitors.'

'Do you have many important visitors?' asked Mma Ramotswe.

'There have been none until now,' he said, 'but it is always possible.'

'Yes,' agreed Mma Ramotswe. 'One never knows.'

She looked over her shoulder, towards a door that led into the rest of the house.

'The other rooms are that way?' she asked politely.

'That is the not-so-tidy part of the house,' said Mr JLB Matekoni. 'Perhaps we should look at it some other time.'

Mma Ramotswe shook her head and Mr JLB Matekoni realised that there could be no secrets in a marriage.

'This way,' he said. 'Really, I must get a better maid.'

Mma Ramotswe followed him. They came to a room with its floor covered in newspapers. In the middle of the floor there was an engine. Around the engine were parts that had been taken from it.

'This is a very special engine,' said Mr JLB Matekoni. 'One day I shall finish fixing it.'

The bathroom was clean but very plain. There was a large bar of carbolic soap on the edge of the bath.

'Carbolic soap is very good for health,' said Mr JLB Matekoni. 'I have always used it.'

The dining room had a table and one chair, but its floor was dirty. There were piles of dust under the furniture and in each corner.

'What does the maid do?' wondered Mma Ramotswe.

'The maid cooks for me,' said Mr JLB Matekoni. 'She makes a meal each day, and it is always the same meal. But she always seems to need a lot of money to buy food and kitchen things.'

'She is very lazy,' said Mma Ramotswe. 'If all the women in Botswana were like her, there would be no men left alive.'

Mr JLB Matekoni smiled. He was not brave enough to get rid of his maid, but now she would have to face Mma Ramotswe.

They were sitting in the living room when they heard a noise.

'That is the maid,' said Mr JLB Matekoni. 'She always closes the kitchen door very loudly when she arrives.'

'Let's go and see her,' said Mma Ramotswe. 'I want to meet this lady.'

Mr JLB Matekoni led the way into the kitchen. A tall woman stood in front of the kitchen sink, filling a pot with water. She was thinner than Mma Ramotswe, but she looked stronger. Mr JLB Matekoni cleared his throat and the woman turned round slowly.

'I am busy ...' she started to say, but stopped when she saw Mma Ramotswe.

Mr JLB Matekoni greeted her politely and introduced his guest.

'Florence, this is Mma Ramotswe,' he said.

'I am glad to meet you, Mma,' said Mma Ramotswe. 'I have heard about you from Mr JLB Matekoni.'

'I am glad that he speaks of me,' said the maid. 'But I am very busy. There is much to do in this house.'

'Yes, a dirty house like this needs a lot of work,' said Mma Ramotswe.

The maid looked offended. 'Why do you say this house is dirty?' she asked.

'Because I have seen it,' said Mma Ramotswe. 'I have seen

'Why do you say this house is dirty?'

the dust in the dining room and the rubbish in the garden.'

The maid's eyes opened wide. 'Who is this woman?' she asked Mr JLB Matekoni angrily. 'Why is she coming into my kitchen and saying things like this?'

Mr JLB Matekoni looked nervous. 'I have asked her to marry me,' he said.

'*Aiee!*' cried the maid. 'You cannot marry her! She will kill you!'

Mr JLB Matekoni put his hand on the maid's shoulder. 'Do not worry, Florence. Mma Ramotswe is a good woman, and I will help you get another job. My cousin has a hotel near the bus station. He needs maids and he can give you a job.'

'I do not want to work in a hotel,' said the maid. 'I am a high-class maid who works in private houses. Oh, oh! I am finished now. If you marry this fat woman, you are finished too. She will break your bed and you will die very quickly.'

Mr JLB Matekoni was embarrassed by the maid's words. He would speak to his cousin as soon as possible, he thought. He and Mma Ramotswe went back to the living room and closed the door behind them.

'Your maid is a difficult woman,' said Mma Ramotswe.

'She is not easy,' said Mr JLB Matekoni. 'But I think we have no choice. She must go to that other job.'

Mma Ramotswe agreed. The maid must go. But she knew that they could not live in this house, either. They would rent it to someone and live in her house in Zebra Drive. Her maid was much better than his and she would take good care of Mr JLB Matekoni. But she had to be careful not to offend him. She would explain that her house was very convenient for the centre of town. That is what she would say. She looked round the room. Was there anything they needed to move from this house to hers? The answer, she thought, was probably no. Mr JLB Matekoni needed only his clothes and his carbolic soap. That was all.

Chapter 2   The Boy with an African Heart

On Monday morning, Mma Ramotswe opened the No. 1 Ladies' Detective Agency. The sign outside the agency said that the opening hours were nine to five, and Mma Ramotswe felt that it was important to keep promises. Actually, clients came only in the late morning or afternoon. Mma Ramotswe was not sure why. Perhaps it took time for people to become brave enough to enter her door and tell her their problems.

So Mma Ramotswe sat with her secretary, Mma Makutsi, and drank the large cup of bush tea* that Mma Makutsi made every morning. She did not really need a secretary, but Mma Makutsi, who had received top marks in her secretarial examinations, was friendly and loyal. Most important of all, she could keep a secret. Mma Ramotswe had found this pleasantly surprising, since most people in Botswana like to talk.

They were not busy that morning. Mma Makutsi cleaned her typewriter and Mma Ramotswe wrote a letter to her cousin in Lobatse. By twelve o'clock she was ready to close the agency for lunch when her secretary suddenly put a piece of paper into her typewriter and began typing quickly. This meant that a client had arrived.

A thin white woman stepped out of a large car in front of the agency. Mma Makutsi let her into the office, and Mma Ramotswe stood up to welcome her.

'I'm sorry, I haven't got an appointment,' said the woman.

'You don't need one,' said Mma Ramotswe, reaching out to shake her hand.

The woman took her hand in the correct Botswana way, Mma Ramotswe noted. She had learned something about how to behave.

---

* bush tea: a South African tea made from red leaves

'I'm Mrs Andrea Curtin,' said the woman as she sat down. 'The American Embassy said you might be able to help me.'

Mma Ramotswe smiled. 'I am glad they suggested me. What do you need?'

'I'm trying to find out what happened to my son, ten years ago,' said Mrs Curtin. 'I don't think he is alive but I want to know what happened.'

For a few moments there was a silence. Then Mma Ramotswe said, 'I am very sorry. I know what it is like to lose a child. I lost my baby. He did not live.'

Mrs Curtin looked down. 'Then you know,' she said.

Mma Makutsi brought two cups of bush tea. Mrs Curtin took her cup gratefully.

'I should tell you about myself,' she said. 'If you can help me, I will be very pleased. If not, I will understand.'

'I cannot help everybody,' said Mma Ramotswe. 'I will tell you if I can help.'

Mrs Curtin began her story.

♦

I came to Africa twelve years ago. My husband, Jack, worked for the World Bank and they gave him a job in Africa for two years. We came with our son Michael, who was eighteen. He had planned to go to college, but we decided that he could spend a year with us in Africa first.

The Bank put us in a house with a beautiful garden in Gaborone. Michael was like a child with a new toy. He got up early in the morning and walked around in the bush before breakfast. I went with him once or twice. He knew the names of all the animals we saw. We watched the sun come up on the edge of the Kalahari Desert and felt its warmth.

I had never been happier in my life. We had found a country where the people had a wonderful feeling for others. When I first heard African people calling each other their brother or sister, it sounded odd to me. But I soon knew what they meant. One day somebody called me her sister and I started to cry.

Michael started to study Setswana and he made good progress. His teacher said to me, 'Your son has got an African heart. I am only teaching that heart to speak.'

After a few months, Michael began to spend time with a group of people who lived on an old farm outside Molepolole. I suppose you could call it a commune. There was a girl from South Africa, a German man named Burkhardt, and some local people. They were all very serious about growing vegetables in dry ground. They sold their vegetables to hotels and hospitals in Gaborone.

One day Michael told me he wanted to live with them. At first I was worried, but I knew it was important for Michael. So I drove him to the farm one Sunday afternoon and left him there.

The farm was only an hour away and they came to Gaborone every day to sell or buy things, so we saw Michael often. He seemed so happy.

When it was time for Michael to return to America for college, he said he did not want to go. He wanted to stay in Botswana for another year. I was upset at first. But Jack and I talked about it and decided to accept what Michael wanted. 'He's doing good work,' Jack said. 'Most young people are completely selfish, but Michael isn't.' I had to agree.

So Michael stayed where he was, and when it was time for us to leave Botswana, he refused to go with us. I was not surprised. The farm was growing. It gave work to twenty families. And Michael was now in love with the South African woman.

Michael wrote to us every week. Then, one week, the letter did not arrive, and a day or two later there was a call from the American Embassy in Botswana. My son was missing. I came back to Botswana immediately and a man from the Embassy

9

met me at the airport. He said that Burkhardt had told the police that Michael had disappeared one evening after supper.

I went to the farm on the day I arrived. Burkhardt said he was sure Michael would appear soon. The South African woman had no idea where Michael was. She did not seem to like me. Neither of them could imagine why Michael would disappear.

I stayed for four weeks. We put a notice in the newspapers and offered a reward for information about my son. A game tracker searched for him for two weeks. We found nothing. Most people decided that Michael had either been killed by robbers or taken by wild animals.

Six months ago Jack died and I decided to try one more time. I know it was ten years ago. I do not think I will find Michael. But I want to know what happened. I would like to be able to say goodbye. Will you help me, Mma Ramotswe? You say that you lost your child. You know how I feel, don't you? It is a sadness that never goes away.

♦

For a few minutes after Mrs Curtin had finished her story, Mma Ramotswe sat in silence. What could she do for this woman, if the Botswana Police and the American Embassy had failed? But the woman needed help, and if she could not get help from the No. 1 Ladies' Detective Agency, then where could she get it?

'I will help you,' she said, and added, 'my sister.'

Chapter 3   The Orphan Farm

Mr JLB Matekoni looked out of the window of his office at Tlokweng Road Speedy Motors. The window looked into the garage, where his assistants were working on a car. They were doing it the wrong way, he noticed, although he had shown them the correct way many times. One of the assistants had already had an accident while he was working on an engine. He had almost lost a finger. But they still worked in an unsafe way. 'Young men think they will never die. But they will find out later,' thought Mr JLB Matekoni. 'They will discover that they are just like the rest of us.'

The assistants always had their lunch under a tree by the road. They sat and ate and watched the girls walk past. Mr JLB Matekoni had heard what they said to the girls.

'You're a pretty girl! Have you got a car? I could fix your car. I could make you go much faster!'

'You're too thin! You're not eating enough meat! A girl like you needs more meat so she can have lots of children!'

Mr JLB Matekoni was shocked. He had never behaved like that when he was young. But this was the way that young men behaved now. You could not stop them. He had tried talking to them about it. He said that if they behaved badly, people would think badly of the garage. They had stared at him, not understanding. They thought people could do whatever they wanted. That was the modern way of thinking.

Mr JLB Matekoni looked at his diary. It was the day he always went to the orphan farm. If he left immediately, he could be back in time to check his young assistants' work. They were only doing simple work on two cars, but sometimes they liked to make the car engines run too fast.

'We are not supposed to make fast cars,' he had told his assistants. 'Our customers are not speedy types like you.'

'Then why are we called Speedy Motors?' asked one assistant.

'Because our *work* is speedy', he answered. 'Our customers do not have to wait a long time.'

He drove to the orphan farm. He enjoyed going there because he liked to see the children, and he usually brought sweets for them. But he also enjoyed seeing Mma Potokwane, the woman who ran the orphan farm. She was an old family friend, and he always fixed things at the farm for her. He was not paid for this, of course. Everybody helped the orphan farm if they could.

He arrived and parked under a tree. Several children had already appeared, and walked beside him on the way to the farm's office.

'Have you children been good?' asked Mr JLB Matekoni.

'We have been very good,' said the oldest child. 'We are tired now from all the good things we have been doing.'

Mr JLB Matekoni laughed and gave them some sweets. Inside the office he found Mma Potokwane. She told him there was a problem with the water pump. Then there was a short silence.

'I hear that you have some news,' she said. 'I hear that you are getting married.'

Mr JLB Matekoni looked down at his shoes. How did she know? It was the maid, he thought. She had told another maid and now everybody knew.

'I am marrying Mma Ramotswe,' he began. 'She …'

'She's the detective lady, isn't she?' said Mma Potokwane. 'I have heard about her. Your life will be exciting. You will be hiding and watching people all the time.'

'I am not going to be a detective,' said Mr JLB Matekoni. 'That is Mma Ramotswe's business.'

♦

After tea, Mr JLB Matekoni went to fix the water pump. It was in a pump-house by some trees. He put down his tool box and opened the pump-house door carefully. Snakes liked machines, and he had often found them in places like this.

Inside the pump-house, he inspected the engine that drove the pump. The problem was that it was very old. He could change some of the parts, but one day Mma Potokwane would have to buy a new one.

There was a noise behind him that surprised him. It sounded like the sound of a wheel that needed oil. Then he saw it, coming out of the bush: a wheelchair, in which a girl was sitting and pushing herself.

She greeted him politely, saying, 'I hope you are well, Rra*.'

They shook hands in the correct way. 'I hope my hands are not too oily,' said Mr JLB Matekoni. 'I have been working on the pump.'

The girl smiled. 'I have brought you some water, Rra. Mma Potokwane said you might be thirsty.'

Mr JLB Matekoni took the water gratefully and watched the girl as he drank. She was very young, about eleven or twelve, and she had a pleasant, open face.

'Do you live on the farm?' he asked.

'I have been here about one year,' she answered. 'I am here with my young brother. He is only five.'

'Where did you come from?'

She looked down. 'We came from near Francistown. My mother died five years ago, when I was seven.'

Mr JLB Matekoni said nothing. Mma Potokwane had told him the stories of some of the orphans, and each time he felt a pain in his heart.

In the old times there were no unwanted children; everybody was cared for by somebody. But things were changing. Now there were orphans, especially because of the disease that was spreading through Africa. Is this what had happened to the girl? And why was she in a wheelchair?

'Your chair is making a noise,' he said. 'Does it always do that?'

The girl shook her head. 'It started a few weeks ago. I think there is something wrong with it.'

* Rra: *Sir* or *Mr* in Setswana

13

Mr JLB Matekoni looked carefully at the wheels.

Mr JLB Matekoni looked carefully at the wheels. It was clear that they needed oil.

'I will lift you out,' he said. 'You can sit under the tree while I fix your chair.'

He put the girl gently on the ground. Then he turned the chair upside down and put oil on the wheels. He turned the chair over and pushed it to where the girl was sitting.

'You have been very kind, Rra,' she said. 'I must go back now, or the house mother will be worried.'

She left, and Mr JLB Matekoni continued his work on the pump. In an hour it was ready, but he knew the repair would not last long. How would the farm get water if the pump stopped working?

Chapter 4   The Commune

Mma Ramotswe sat in her office at the No. 1 Ladies' Detective Agency and examined the ring on her left hand. The assistant in Judgement Day Jewellers had wanted Mr JLB Matekoni to spend a lot of pula* on an engagement ring with a much bigger diamond. But Mma Ramotswe was not interested in the size of the stone. A tear ran down her face as she thought of the man she would marry. Nobody had ever given her anything like that ring before, she thought. He would be a good husband for her and she would try to be a good wife for him.

She shook her head and turned her thoughts to the day's business – Mrs Curtin's case. She did not really want to look for the son. Why look for information about the past if it would only bring unhappiness?

But since she had agreed to help, she should start at the

* pula: the money of Botswana

beginning. This was the commune where Burkhardt and his friends had started their farm. She probably would not discover anything, but she might get a feeling for what had happened.

At least she knew where to find the commune. It was near Silokwolela, a village in the west, not far from Molepolole. She left early on Saturday morning in her little white van. There was already a stream of traffic, mostly people coming into town for shopping. But a few people were leaving town as well. Mma Ramotswe slowed down. There was a woman at the side of the road waving her hand for a ride.

Mma Ramotswe stopped her van and called out, 'Where are you going, Mma?'

'To Silokwolela,' said the woman, pointing down the road.

'I am going there too. I can take you all the way.'

'You are very kind, and I am very lucky,' said the woman.

As they travelled, Mma Ramotswe spoke with the woman, who was called Mma Tsbago. She knew a little about the farm. People had thought it would be a success, but it had failed. Mma Tsbago was not surprised at that. People often give up if things are too difficult.

'Is there somebody in your village who can take me to the farm?' asked Mma Ramotswe.

Mma Tsbago thought for a moment. 'Yes, there is a friend of my uncle who had a job there.'

When they arrived at Silokwolela, Mma Tsbago took Mma Ramotswe to a well-kept house on the edge of the village. They waited at the gate while Mma Tsbago called out, 'Mma Potsane, I am here to see you!'

A small, round woman came out and let them in.

Mma Tsbago explained to her why they were there.

'Yes,' said Mma Potsane, 'my husband and I both worked out there. But then things went wrong. People stopped believing in what they were doing, and went away.'

'Was there an American boy?' asked Mma Ramotswe.

'He disappeared. The police came and looked for him. His mother came too, many times. One time she brought a game tracker. He was a little man and he ran round like a dog. He looked under stones and smelled the air, but he found no sign that wild animals had taken the boy.'

'What do you think happened to him?' asked Mma Ramotswe.

'I think he was blown away by the wind and put down somewhere far away. Maybe in the middle of the Kalahari.'

Mma Tsbago looked at Mma Ramotswe, but Mma Ramotswe looked straight ahead at Mma Potsane.

'That is possible, Mma,' she said. 'Could you take me out to the farm? I can give you twenty pula.'

'Of course,' said Mma Potsane. 'I do not like to go there at night, but in the day it is different.'

Mma Tsbago went to her home, and Mma Ramotswe and Mma Potsane left the village in the little white van. The dirt road was rough and Mma Ramotswe had to drive slowly.

The road ended, and Mma Ramotswe stopped the van under a tree. There had probably been eleven or twelve houses at one time, but now most of them had fallen down. She and Mma Potsane walked to the main farm house. It still had a roof and doors, and glass in some of the windows.

'That is where the German lived, and the American and the South African woman,' said Mma Potsane.

'I should like to go inside,' said Mma Ramotswe.

They entered the house, feeling the cooler air.

'You see, there is nothing here,' said Mma Potsane.

Mma Ramotswe was not listening. She was studying a piece of yellowing paper which had been pinned to a wall. It was a newspaper photograph – a picture of some people standing in front of a building.

She pointed to one of the people in the photograph. 'Who is this man, Mma?' she asked.

Mma Potsane looked closely at the photograph. 'I remember him. He worked here too. He came from Francistown. His father was a schoolteacher and this one, the son, was very clever. He was friendly with the American, but the German didn't like him.'

Mma Ramotswe gently put the photograph into her pocket. They went through the other rooms of the house. Some of them had no roofs, and the floors were covered with leaves. It was an empty house – except for the photograph.

Mma Potsane was pleased to leave the house, and showed Mma Ramotswe the place where they had grown vegetables. The land had become wild again. All the wooden fences had been eaten by the ants. Only the ditches were left, old and unused.

'All that work,' said Mma Ramotswe. 'And now this.'

'But this always happens,' said Mma Potsane. 'Even in Gaborone. How do we know that Gaborone will still be here fifty years from now? Perhaps the ants have plans for Gaborone as well.'

Mma Ramotswe smiled. 'Will the No. 1 Ladies' Detective Agency be remembered twenty years from now?' she wondered. 'Or Tlokweng Road Speedy Motors?' Probably not, she decided, but was that very important?

She had come here for information about something that had happened many years ago, and she had found nothing, or almost nothing. It seemed that the wind had blown everything away.

She turned to Mma Potsane.

'Where does the wind come from, Mma?' she asked.

'Over there,' Mma Potsane said, pointing to the trees and the empty sky, to the Kalahari. 'Over there.'

Mma Ramotswe said nothing. She felt that she was very close to understanding what had happened, but she did not know why.

Chapter 5   The Children's Story

On the day that Mma Ramotswe travelled to Silokwolela, Mr JLB Matekoni felt uncomfortable. He usually met Mma Ramotswe on Saturday mornings to help her with shopping or work around her house. Without her, Gaborone seemed empty. He decided he would visit Mma Potokwane at the orphan farm again. She was always happy to sit down and talk about things over a cup of tea.

Mma Potokwane greeted him as he parked his car.

'I am very glad that you came today,' said Mma Potokwane. 'I was going to phone you.'

'Is it your car? Or the water pump?' asked Mr JLB Matekoni.

'The pump. It is making a strange noise. It seems to be in pain.'

'Engines feel pain. They tell us by making a noise.'

'Then the pump needs help,' said Mma Potokwane. 'Can you look at it?'

'Of course,' said Mr JLB Matekoni.

It took him a long time, but at last he was able to fix the pump. It would need to be changed one day, but at least the noise had stopped.

Back in Mma Potokwane's office, he had a cup of tea and a piece of cake that the farm cooks had baked that morning. The orphans were well fed, unlike many in other African countries. Botswana was fortunate. Everyone had enough to eat.

'So you will be married soon,' said Mma Potokwane. 'You will have to behave yourself, Mr JLB Matekoni!'

He laughed, eating the last piece of his cake. 'Mma Ramotswe will watch me. She will make sure that I behave well.'

'Will you live in her house or yours?' asked Mma Potokwane.

'I think we will live in her house,' he said. 'It is a bit nicer than mine. It is in Zebra Drive, you know.'

'Yes, I have seen it,' said Mma Potokwane. 'It's quite big, isn't it? There will be room for children.'

'We have not been thinking of that,' said Mr JLB Matekoni. 'We are probably too old for children.'

Mr JLB Matekoni wondered if he would have the energy to take care of children. He wanted to fix engines during the day and spend his evenings with Mma Ramotswe. Children needed to be taken to school and put in the bath and taken to the hospital. Would he and Mma Ramotswe really want that?

'Of course,' said Mma Potokwane, watching him as she spoke, 'you could take an orphan as a foster child. You could give the children to Mma Ramotswe as a wedding gift. Women love children.'

'But ...'

Mma Potokwane interrupted. 'There are two children who would be happy to live with you.'

'Two children? Two?'

'A brother and a sister. We do not want to separate them. The girl is twelve and the boy is five. Actually, you have met one of them already. The girl in the wheelchair.'

Mr JLB Matekoni said nothing. He remembered the child, who had been very polite and grateful. But would it not be rather difficult to look after a child in a wheelchair? Mma Potokwane had said nothing about this when she began talking about children. Then she had added an extra child – the brother – and now she appeared to believe that the wheelchair was not important. He stopped himself. He could be the one in that chair.

Mma Potokwane had been looking out of the window. Now she turned to him.

'Would you like me to call that child?' she asked. 'I am not trying to force you, Mr JLB Matekoni, but would you like to meet her again, and the little boy?'

The room was silent. Mr JLB Matekoni remembered how it was to be a child, back in the village, all those years ago. He remembered how the village mechanic had let him clean lorries and mend tyres, and by this kindness had helped him find his life's work. It was easy to make a difference in people's lives.

'Call them,' he said. 'I would like to see them.'

'You are a good man, Mr JLB Matekoni,' she said. 'I will ask someone to bring them here. They are in the fields now. But while we are waiting, I will tell you their story.'

◆

The Basarwa*, said Mma Potokwane, lead a hard life in the Kalahari. They have no cows, no houses to live in. When you wonder how you and I could live like that, you will know that these bushmen are special people.

A group of bushmen had come from the Kalahari to a village near Maun, hunting game. They had a camp a few kilometres outside the village. They had killed some animals and had plenty of meat, so they were happy to stay there, sleeping under the bushes.

There were several children, and one woman had just given birth to a baby boy. She was sleeping with him at her side, away from the others. She had a daughter, too, who was sleeping on the other side of her mother. While the mother was sleeping, a snake bit her. She died before the baby woke up.

The bushmen prepared to bury the mother that morning. But when a bushman woman dies, and she is still feeding a baby, they bury the baby too. There just isn't enough food for a baby without a mother.

---

* Basarwa: the people who live in the Kalahari Desert. They are also called bushmen.

The girl hid in the bush and watched them take her mother and her baby brother. They dug a shallow hole in the sand and put the mother in it. The other women cried and the men sang. The girl watched as they put her little brother in the hole too. Then they pushed sand over them both and went back to the camp.

The moment they had gone, the girl came out and started digging. Soon she had her brother in her arms. There was sand in his nose but he was still breathing. She ran through the bush to the road. A short time later, a Government lorry came past and stopped. The driver was probably surprised to see a girl standing at the side of the road with a baby in her arms. He couldn't understand what she said, but he took her to a hospital on the way to Francistown.

The baby was thin and the girl had TB, which was not unusual. They kept the children in the hospital for two months and gave the girl drugs. Then they let them go because beds in the TB rooms were needed for other sick people.

A nurse at the hospital was worried about the children, so she took them to her home and let them live in a small room. The nurse and her husband fed the children, but they had two children of their own and not much money.

The girl learned the Setswana language quickly. She discovered how to earn a few pula by collecting empty bottles from the side of the road and taking them back to the bottle shop. Sometimes she asked for money outside the railway station, but she preferred to earn it if she could. And although she was still a child herself, she was a good mother to the baby boy. She washed him and made clothes for him. She always carried him on her back and never let him out of her sight.

This went on for four years. Then the girl became ill. They took her back to the hospital and found that the TB had badly damaged her bones. After some time, she could not walk. The nurse found a wheelchair for her. Now she had to look after the boy from the wheelchair, and he did little things to help his sister.

The nurse and her husband had to move. The husband had a new job down in Lobatse. The nurse knew about the orphan farm, so she wrote to me. I said that we would take them, and I went to Francistown to get them just a few months ago. Now they are here with us, as you have seen.

That is their story, Mr JLB Matekoni. That is how they came here.

♦

Mr JLB Matekoni said nothing. He looked at Mma Potokwane. The children's story had affected him deeply.

'They will be here in a few minutes,' said Mma Potokwane. 'Do you want me to say that you might be able to take them?'

Mr JLB Matekoni closed his eyes. He had not spoken to Mma Ramotswe about it and it seemed wrong to surprise her with something like this. Was this a good way to start their marriage?

But here were the children. The girl in her wheelchair, smiling at him, and the boy standing there, looking so serious.

He took a deep breath. There were times in life when a person had to do something. This was probably one of those times.

'Would you children like to come and stay with me?' he said. 'Just for a week or two? Then we can see how things are.'

The girl looked at Mma Potokwane.

'Rra Matekoni will look after you well,' she said. 'You will be happy there.'

The girl turned to her brother and said something to him that the adults did not hear. The boy thought for a moment, and then smiled.

'You are very kind, Rra,' the girl said. 'We will be happy to come with you.'

Mma Potokwane shouted happily. 'Go and pack, children,' she said. 'Take some clean clothes.'

The girl turned her wheelchair round and left the room with her brother.

'What have I done?' asked Mr JLB Matekoni quietly.

'A very good thing,' Mma Potokwane said.

Chapter 6   Mma Makutsi's Promotion

Mma Makutsi, Secretary of the No. 1 Ladies' Detective Agency and top graduate of the Botswana Secretarial College, sat at her desk and looked out of the open door. She liked to leave the door open but sometimes the chickens came in. She did not like the chickens. It was not professional to have chickens in a detective agency.

'Get out,' said Mma Makutsi. 'This is not a chicken farm. Out.' She got up and the chickens moved slowly towards the door.

How many top graduates of the Botswana Secretarial College had to push chickens out of their offices, she wondered. She had expected to get a job in one of the modern office buildings in town, but she had received no offers. But some women with much worse marks on the examination had found good jobs. Why?

'Men run these businesses, don't they?' said one of the other students in Mma Makutsi's class.

'I suppose so,' said Mma Makutsi. 'Men choose the secretaries.'

'So how do you think they choose them? By their examination marks? Of course not! Men choose the beautiful girls. To the others, they say, "Sorry, but all the jobs have gone".'

Mma Makutsi had cried that evening. Why had she worked so hard for her top marks? Would she ever get a job at all?

The next day the question was answered. She was offered the job of secretary at Mma Ramotswe's agency. If men will not give you a job, go to a woman. The office was not modern, it was true, but it was certainly better to work in a detective agency than in a bank or a lawyer's office.

But there was still this problem with the chickens.

♦

'So, Mma Makutsi,' said Mma Ramotswe, 'I went to Molepolole and found the commune where those people lived. I spoke to a woman who had worked there and I saw everything there was to see.'

'And you found something?' asked Mma Makutsi, making a pot of bush tea.

'I found a feeling,' said Mma Ramotswe. 'I felt that the young American was there.'

'He is still living there?'

'No. He is dead. But he is there.'

Mma Makutsi understood. When we die, we do not leave the place where we were living. A part of us never goes away.

She poured the tea and gave a cup to Mma Ramotswe.

'Are you going to tell the American woman this?' she asked. 'She will ask, "Where is the body?" She won't understand.'

Mma Ramotswe looked at her secretary. 'This is an intelligent person,' she thought. 'She knows how the American woman would think.'

'I also found this,' said Mma Ramotswe. She took the newspaper photograph out of her pocket and gave it to Mma Makutsi. 'It was on the wall. Those people lived there at the time.'

'There are names below the photograph,' said Mma Makutsi. 'Cephas Kalumani. Mma Soloi. Oswald Ranta. But even if we find these people, what can they tell us? I'm sure the police talked to them. Maybe they even spoke to Mma Curtin.'

Mma Makutsi studied the people in the photograph. Two men and a woman were standing in the front. Another man and woman were behind them, their faces unclear.

The names belonged to the people in the front. Cephas Kalumani was a tall, thin man who looked uncomfortable. Mma Soloi, next to him, was smiling – a hard-working, uncomplaining woman.

The third person was Oswald Ranta. He was good-looking and well dressed, with a white shirt and tie. Like Mma Soloi, he was smiling. But his smile was very different.

'I do not like Ranta,' said Mma Makutsi. 'I do not like the way he looks.'

'I know,' said Mma Ramotswe. 'That is a bad man.'

'Are you going to find him?'

'That is the next thing I shall do. But first you can help me with some letters.'

While Mma Makutsi typed the letters, she thought about Oswald Ranta. His name was slightly unusual. It would be simple to look the name up in the telephone book. When she finished the letter, she took out the Botswana telephone book. As she thought, there was only one Oswald Ranta.

While Mma Ramotswe was signing the letters, Mma Makutsi called the number. 'Is Rra Ranta there, please?' she asked. She spoke in a low voice and Mma Ramotswe did not hear her.

'He is at work at the university,' said a woman's voice. 'I am his maid.'

'I'm sorry, Mma, but I have to phone him at work. Can you give me the number?'

She wrote the number on a piece of paper. Then she made another telephone call and again wrote something on the paper.

'Mma Ramotswe,' she said when she was finished, 'Oswald Ranta is living here in Gaborone. He teaches at the university. His secretary says he comes in at eight o'clock every morning.'

Mma Makutsi studied the people in the photograph.

Mma Ramotswe smiled. 'You are very clever. How did you find all this out?'

'I looked in the telephone book. Then I called to find out the rest.'

'That was very good detective work.'

'I am happy that you think so. I want to be a detective.'

Mma Ramotswe thought about her secretary. She was intelligent and a good worker. Why not give her a promotion and make her happy? They could buy an answering machine to answer the telephone.

'I will give you a promotion,' said Mma Ramotswe. 'You will be an assistant detective. Starting tomorrow.'

Mma Makutsi stood up. She opened her mouth to speak but no words came out. The emotion was too great.

Chapter 7   Mr Badule's Wife

It was the first day of Mma Makutsi's promotion to assistant detective.

'You are an assistant detective,' Mma Ramotswe had said, 'but you will still need to type and do other things.'

'That is all right,' said Mma Makutsi. 'I can do all those things, but I will do more as well. I shall have clients.'

Mma Ramotswe was surprised. She had not planned on letting Mma Makutsi have her own clients. But maybe it was selfish to keep all the clients for herself.

'Yes,' she said. 'You can have clients. But not the big clients at first. You can start with small matters.'

'That is quite fair,' said Mma Makutsi. 'I do not want to run before I can walk. Thank you, Mma.'

Mma Ramotswe thought she should give Mma Makutsi a client as soon as possible. When, later that morning, Mr

Letsenyane Badule arrived, she decided that this would be her assistant's first case.

Mr Badule was nervous as he sat in the client's chair.

'You need not feel embarrassed,' said Mma Ramotswe. 'Many people come here to ask for help.'

'Actually,' said Mma Makutsi, 'it is the strong people who ask for help. The weak ones are too ashamed to ask.'

Mr Badule seemed to relax after Mma Makutsi said this. That was good, thought Mma Ramotswe. She knows how to speak to a client.

'I have been very worried,' said Mr Badule. 'I have not been able to sleep. I have a question that keeps me awake.'

'Why don't you tell us about yourself, Rra?' said Mma Ramotswe.

Mr Badule told his story over a cup of tea.

♦

I am not an important man, he began. I come from Lobatse, and my father worked at the High Court, as a cleaner. He was a hard worker and the judge was kind to him. He was kind to me too. He helped me get a place in a good school.

When I passed my examinations, I got a job with the Government Meat Agency. I worked hard. When I saw other workers steal meat, I reported it. My boss was pleased with me and gave me a promotion.

After some time, I saved enough money to buy my own shop. Perhaps you have seen it on the road to Lobatse. It is called the Honest Meat Shop.

The shop does quite well, but I have not got a lot of extra money. My wife does not work and she likes expensive clothes.

For many years we did not have children. But then we had a son. I was proud of him.

My son did not do well in school. His teachers said his writing

29

was untidy and full of mistakes. My wife said that we should send him to a private school, but I was worried that it would be too expensive. When I said that, she became very cross.

'If you cannot pay for a private school,' she said, 'I will go to a charity and ask them to pay.'

'There are no charities that will pay for private schools,' I said.

'I know one that will, and I will speak to them tomorrow.'

She went to town the next day. When she came back, she said it had all been arranged. 'The charity will pay for him to go to Thornhill,' she said. 'He can start next term.'

I was surprised. Thornhill is a very good school, you know. I asked my wife to tell me the name of the charity, so I could thank them, but she said that it was a secret.

My son liked Thornhill and soon he was getting good marks in mathematics and writing. I think if he continues to do well, he will get an important job in the Government one day. And he is the grandson of a cleaner!

I'm sure you are thinking, why should this man complain? He has a well-dressed wife and a clever son. But when I come home from work and my wife is not yet home, and I wait until ten or eleven o'clock before she returns, I worry. Because, you see, I think my wife is seeing another man. I know many husbands say that, and they are wrong. I hope I am wrong. But I cannot have any peace until I know if it is true or not.

♦

When Mr Letsenyane Badule left the office, Mma Ramotswe looked at Mma Makutsi and smiled.

'This is a very simple case, Mma Makutsi,' she said. 'I think you should be able to handle it alone.'

'Thank you, Mma Ramotswe,' said Mma Makutsi. 'I shall do my best.'

'So, what do you think?'

'I think Mma Badule is getting money from somewhere. That means she is getting it from a man. She is paying for the school with the money.'

Mma Ramotswe agreed. 'So now you should follow her one day and see where she goes. She should lead you straight to the house of this other man. Find the maid and give her one hundred pula. She will tell you everything. Maids like to talk about what happens in their boss's house. Then you tell Mr Badule.'

'That is the part I will not like,' said Mma Makutsi.

♦

Mma Makutsi felt wonderful. It was her first case as an assistant detective. She could not drive, so she asked her uncle to drive her. He was excited about doing detective work, and put on a pair of dark glasses.

Early the next morning, they drove to the house next to Mr Badule's shop. They found a place to park across the road and waited in the car.

'I have seen many films like this,' said the uncle. 'The detectives sit in their car and wait patiently. Then somebody starts shooting.'

'Nobody will shoot,' said Mma Makutsi. 'There is no shooting in Botswana.'

At seven o'clock a boy came out of the house, dressed in the uniform of the Thornhill School.

'Should I make a note of this?' asked the uncle.

At first Mma Makutsi wanted to say that it would not be necessary, but she changed her mind. It would give her uncle something to do. So the uncle wrote on a piece of paper: 'Badule boy leaves house at 7 AM and goes to school on foot.'

Twenty minutes later, Mr Badule came out of the house and walked over to his shop. The uncle made a note of this too.

They waited for four hours. The car was becoming hot, and Mma Makutsi was becoming annoyed by all the notes her uncle was taking. Then they saw Mma Badule leave the house. She got into a car and began to drive into town.

Mma Makutsi and her uncle followed her to a large house on Nyerere Drive. Mma Badule got out of the car and went inside. Mma Makutsi remembered Mma Ramotswe's advice. The best thing to do would be to talk to the maids and offer them the new fifty pula notes that Mma Ramotswe had given her.

Her uncle wanted to go with her, but Mma Makutsi said it would not be dangerous to talk to a few maids in the middle of the day. He looked nervous as she left the car and went to the maid's entrance. He took out his pencil, looked at his watch and made a note: 'Mma Makutsi enters house at 2:10 PM.'

There were two maids, one of them older than the other. They both stared at Mma Makutsi.

'I want to talk to you, my sisters,' said Mma Makutsi. 'I want to talk about the woman who has come to visit this house.'

'She is a very well-dressed lady,' said the younger maid. 'She comes and sits and drinks tea.'

The older maid smiled. 'But she is also very tired. She often has to lie down to rest in the bedroom.'

The younger one laughed loudly. 'Oh, yes! There is much resting in that bedroom.'

Mma Makutsi laughed too. This was going to be easy.

'Who is the man who lives in this house?' she asked. 'Has he no wife?'

'He has a wife, all right,' said the older maid. 'She lives in their village, near Mahalaype. He goes there at weekends. This woman here is his town wife.'

'Does the village wife know about the town wife?'

'No, she would not like it. She is a religious woman and very rich. She bought this house for her husband.'

'But she does not like to live in Gaborone,' added the younger maid. 'She prefers her village. So he has to go back every Friday, like a schoolboy going home for the weekend.'

'The man said that if we told his wife, we would lose our jobs,' said the older maid. 'So we keep our mouths shut.'

Suddenly both maids looked upset. *'Aiee!'* cried the younger one. 'Have you been sent by the wife?'

'No,' said Mma Makutsi quickly. 'I do not know the wife. The other woman's husband has asked me to find out what she is doing.'

'But if you tell him what is happening,' said the older maid, 'he might tell the real wife. That way we lose our jobs too. And there is a boy who belongs to the well-dressed woman. If you look, you will see that he is the son of the man in this house, not the other man. They both have big noses. The boy comes here every day after school, but does not tell the father that he lives with. That is bad. What will happen to Botswana, Mma, if we teach boys to lie?'

Mma Makutsi returned to her uncle's car. He had fallen asleep. She touched his arm and he woke up.

'Ah! You are safe! I am glad that you are back.'

'We can go now,' said Mma Makutsi. 'I have found out everything I need to know.'

They drove back to the No. 1 Ladies' Detective Agency. Mma Makutsi had not needed to give money to the maids, so she gave fifty pula to her uncle for helping her. Then she sat down to write her report.

The client's wife has been seeing a man for many years. He is the husband of a rich woman who does not know about this. The boy is the son of this man, and not the son of the client. I am not sure what to do, but I think we have two choices.

(a) We tell the client everything. This is what he asked us to do. We have promised to tell him about his wife and we should keep our promises.

(b) We tell the client that there is another man, but we do not know who he is. I do not like to lie, as I believe in God. But if we tell the client everything, he will be sad. He will find out that his son is not his real son. Would God want him to be unhappy? And what if the rich woman finds out? She may stop giving money to the real father and he may stop paying for the boy's school. Then the boy would suffer.

For these reasons, I do not know what to do.

Mma Makutsi signed the report and put it on Mma Ramotswe's desk. Then she looked out of the window at the trees. She had received top marks from the Botswana Secretarial College, but they had not taught her how to answer a question like this one.

Chapter 8   A Trip into Town

On the morning that Mma Makutsi followed Mr Letsenyane Badule's wife to the house of another man, Mr JLB Matekoni decided to take his new children shopping.

The children's arrival at his home had upset him deeply. He had gone out to fix a water pump and had come back with two children. Now he had to take care of them until they were adults – actually, in the case of the girl in the wheelchair, for the rest of her life. How had Mma Potokwane made him do it?

But the children had arrived and now it was too late to change that. As he sat in the office of Tlokweng Road Speedy Motors, he made a decision. He would stop worrying about how the children had arrived, and think only about how to take good care of them. They were fine children and their lives had suddenly become better. Yesterday they had been two of one hundred and fifty children at the orphan farm. Today they were living in a house with their own room, and with a father – he was a father now! – who owned his own business. There was enough money, so why not spend some on the children? They

34

could go to a private school and learn everything they needed to get good jobs.

Perhaps the boy … No, he could not really hope for this, but it was an attractive thought. Perhaps the boy would be interested in mechanical things and could run Tlokweng Speedy Motors. For a few moments, Mr JLB Matekoni imagined his son, his *son*, standing in front of the garage, cleaning his hands on a piece of oily cloth after fixing a complicated engine. And in the background, sitting in the office, he and Mma Ramotswe, much older now, with grey hair, drinking bush tea.

That would be far in the future. There was much to do before that. First, he would take them into town and buy them new clothes. The children had probably never had new clothes before. Then he would take them to the chemist's shop. The girl could buy creams and sweet-smelling soap and other things that girls like. There was only carbolic soap at home, and she deserved better than that.

Mr JLB Matekoni took the old green pick-up truck from the garage. It had plenty of room in the back for the wheelchair. The children were sitting in front of his house. The boy was playing with a stick and the girl was making a cover for a milk bottle. 'She is a clever girl,' he thought. 'She will be able to do anything if she is given a chance.'

They greeted him politely, and said the maid had given them breakfast. He had asked the maid to come in early to take care of the children and she had agreed. But he heard loud noises from the kitchen, and he knew the maid was in a bad mood.

They rode into town. The girl asked questions about the old pick-up, which surprised him.

'I have heard that old engines need more oil,' she said, 'Is this true, Rra?'

He explained about old engine parts and she listened carefully, but the boy did not seem interested.

When they arrived in town, he parked the pick-up next to a big white Range Rover outside the British Embassy.

'Do you see that car? That is a very important car,' he said. 'The owner always takes it to my garage.'

The boy said nothing, but the girl said, 'It is a beautiful white car. It is like a cloud on wheels.'

Mr JLB Matekoni turned round and looked at her.

'That is a very good way of talking about that car,' he said. 'I shall remember that.'

The shop assistants were very kind. They helped the girl try on the dresses she had chosen. They were the cheapest dresses, but she said they were the ones she wanted.

The boy seemed more interested. He chose the brightest shirts he could find. He wanted a pair of white shoes, but his sister disagreed.

'We cannot let him have those shoes, Rra,' she said to Mr JLB Matekoni. 'They will get dirty very quickly and then he will throw them away.'

'I see,' said Mr JLB Matekoni. The boy was polite and well-behaved, but he began to think his son would never stand with an oily cloth outside Tlokweng Speedy Motors. He had another thought of the boy, in a stylish white shirt and a suit.

They finished shopping and were walking past the post office when the photographer stopped them.

'I can take a photograph for you, right here,' he said. 'You stand under this tree and I can take your photograph. You can have it immediately. A handsome family group.'

'Would you like that?' asked Mr JLB Matekoni. 'A photograph to remind us of our shopping trip?'

The children smiled. 'Yes, please,' said the girl. 'I have never had a photograph.'

This girl, thought Mr JLB Matekoni, was twelve years old but she had never had a photograph of herself. There was no photograph of her childhood. Nobody had ever taken her picture. She had not been special enough.

He had a sudden strong feeling of pity for these children, pity mixed with love. He would give them these things. They would have everything that other children had.

He pushed the girl's wheelchair in front of the tree. The photographer waved his hand to get her attention. Then he pushed a button on the camera. There was a noise and then, as if he was performing a magic trick, the photographer pulled out the photograph and gave it to the girl.

She took it and smiled. Then the photographer did the same performance with the boy.

'Now you can put those photographs in your rooms,' said Mr JLB Matekoni. 'And one day we will have more photographs.'

He turned round to push the wheelchair, but he stopped and his arms fell to his sides, useless.

There was Mma Ramotswe, standing in front of him, carrying a basket of letters. She had been on her way to the post office when she saw him. What was happening? What was Mr JLB Matekoni doing, and who were those children?

Chapter 9   The Bad Maid

Florence Peko, the bad-tempered maid of Mr JLB Matekoni, had a headache. She had had headaches since Mr JLB Matekoni said that he was going to marry Mma Ramotswe. Whenever something bad happened, Florence had a headache. When her brother was in court, for example, she had had headaches. When she visited him in prison, there was always a headache.

Her brother had been arrested for stealing cars.

Why did he have to go to prison? There were many other men who were much worse than he was. There was a long list of bad men in Botswana. She knew some of them.

And one of them, Mr Philemon Leannye, might even help her, she thought. She had met him at a restaurant. He was tired of bar girls, he said. He wanted to meet some honest girls who would not take his money.

'Someone like you,' he had said.

He made her feel special, and they began to see each other. He often disappeared for a month or two, but then he returned with a gift for her. A silver clock, a bag, a bottle of wine. He lived with a woman and three children.

'That woman always shouts at me,' he complained. 'I give her money every month, but she always wants more. She says the children are hungry. She is never satisfied.'

'You should leave her and marry me,' said Florence. 'I would not shout at a man. I would make a good wife for a man like you.'

She had been serious, but he laughed.

'You would be just as bad,' he said. 'When women marry, they start to complain. Everyone knows this.'

Then one time, when he was in trouble, the police talked to her. She told them that he was with her when he was not. Now he would have to do something for her.

One hot afternoon, they were in Mr JLB Matekoni's bedroom. 'Philemon,' she said to him, 'I want a gun. Can you get one for me?'

He laughed. 'Who do you want to shoot? Mr JLB Matekoni? Do you want to shoot him the next time he complains about your cooking? Hah!'

'No, I am not going to shoot anybody. I want to put the gun in someone's house. Then I will tell the police about the gun and they will come and find it.'

'So I won't get my gun back?'

'No. The police will take it. But they will also take the person who lives in the house. What happens if the police find a gun that you are not supposed to have?'

Philemon lit a cigarette and blew smoke towards Mr JLB Matekoni's ceiling.

'The police don't want people to have guns here,' he said. 'If they catch you with a gun, you go to prison.'

'I am glad to hear that,' said Florence.

'So how will I pay for this gun?' he asked. 'It will cost five hundred pula – maybe more. Someone has to go to South Africa to get one. You can't buy them in Botswana.'

'I haven't got five hundred pula,' she said. 'Why not steal the gun? You know where you can get one. Ask one of your boys to do it.' She paused, and then said, 'Remember that I helped you. That was not easy for me.'

He looked at her carefully. 'Do you really want this?'

'Yes,' she said. 'It's really important to me.'

He put out his cigarette.

'All right,' he said. 'I'll get you a gun. But remember, if anything goes wrong, you did not get the gun from me.'

'I shall say I found it,' said Florence. 'I shall say that it was lying in the bush near the prison. Maybe one of the prisoners left it there.'

'That sounds good,' said Philemon. 'When do you want it?'

'As soon as you can get it.' she replied.

'I can get you one tonight,' he said. 'Actually, I have an extra one. You can have that.'

She touched him gently. 'You are a very kind man. You can come and see me any time. I am always happy to see you, and make you happy.'

'You are a very fine girl,' he said, laughing. 'Very bad. Very clever.'

◆

39

He gave her the gun, as he had promised. It was inside a paper package at the bottom of a white shopping bag. She took it out of the package and he started to explain how to use it, but she interrupted.

'I am not interested in that,' she said. 'All I am interested in is this gun, and the bullets.'

He gave her some bullets. She liked the way they felt. They would make fine jewellery, she thought, if you put them together on a string.

Philemon helped her to put the bullets into the gun, and to clean the gun afterwards so there would be no marks from her fingers. Then he kissed her and left. She missed him as soon as he had gone. If she went to his house and shot his wife, she wondered, would he marry her?

But she could never shoot anyone. She was a good person, she thought. She just had bad luck. That's why she had to do things that good people did not do. Or said they did not do – Florence knew that everybody did bad things sometimes. And she was only trying to save Mr JLB Matekoni from that fat detective woman, who shouldn't try to take what wasn't hers. A few years in prison would teach that woman a lesson.

'I have got a gun,' thought Florence. 'Now I need to put the gun into a house in Zebra Drive.'

She needed someone else to help her. Fortunately, a man called Paul had borrowed money from her two years ago. It was not a lot of money, but he had never paid it back. Perhaps he had forgotten about it, but Florence had not forgotten, and now she would remind him. And Paul had a wife who did not know about his secret visits to Mr JLB Matekoni's house. If he refused, she could say she was going to tell the wife.

When she reminded him of the money, Paul said he could not pay it back.

'My wife knows about every pula I spend,' he said. 'One of

He gave her the gun, as he had promised.

our children is always ill. We have to pay the hospital a lot of money. But I will pay you back one day.'

'I can forget the money if you do something for me,' she said. 'Just go to an empty house, break a window in the kitchen and go inside.'

'I am not a robber,' he said. 'I do not steal.'

'I am not asking you to steal. I want you to put something in the house. It's just a package that I want to keep in a safe place.'

At last he agreed. He would do it the next afternoon, when everybody was at work. She knew that the maid would not be there, and there was no dog.

She gave him the package. He did not know what it was, but it was heavy and he began to have doubts.

'Don't ask,' she said. 'Don't ask and you won't know.'

'It's a gun,' he thought. 'She wants me to put a gun in the house in Zebra Drive.'

'I don't want to carry this with me,' he said. 'It's very dangerous. I know it's a gun and I don't want the police to catch me with it. I will fetch it from you at the Matekoni house tomorrow.'

She thought for a moment. She could carry the gun to Mr JLB Matekoni's house in the shopping bag. Paul could take it from her there. The important thing was to put it in the Ramotswe house, and then, two days later, to make that telephone call to the police.

'All right,' she said. 'Come at 2.30 tomorrow. He will be at the garage then.' She put the package back in the shopping bag. 'You have been a good man. Now I want to make you happy.'

No,' he said. 'I am too nervous to be happy. Maybe some other time.'

♦

The following afternoon, Paul Monosopati, an employee of the

Gaborone Sun Hotel, and a man who was expecting promotion, made a telephone call.

'Now listen to me, Rra,' he said to the man at the other end, 'I cannot speak for long. But I am against crime.'

'That's good,' said the policeman.

'If you go to a house on the way to the old airport, you will find a woman with a gun. She sells them. You will catch her if you go now. The gun does not belong to the man who owns the house, it is the woman's gun. She will have it with her in the kitchen, in a white shopping bag.'

He gave the address of the house and then put down the telephone. At the other end of the line, the policeman smiled. This would be an easy arrest, he thought. There should be a reward for good citizens who reported crimes like this, he thought. Five hundred pula, at least.

Chapter 10   Family

Mr JLB Matekoni looked up at the empty sky. Then he looked down. Mma Ramotswe was still there, not understanding what she saw. She knew that he worked for the orphan farm. She would think he was taking two orphans out for the day. She would not imagine that he had two foster children, and that they would soon be her foster children too.

'What are you doing?' she said simply.

It was a reasonable question. Mr JLB Matekoni looked at the children. The girl had put her photograph into the plastic bag on the side of her wheelchair. The boy was holding his photograph tightly, afraid, perhaps, that Mma Ramotswe would take it away from him.

'These are two children from the orphan farm,' said Mr JLB Matekoni with a weak voice.

The girl smiled and greeted Mma Ramotswe politely.

'I am called Motholeli,' she said. 'My brother is called Puso. These are the names that we were given at the orphan farm.'

'I hope they are looking after you well,' said Mma Ramotswe. 'Mma Potokwane is a kind lady.'

'She is kind,' said the girl. 'Very kind.'

Mr JLB Matekoni spoke quickly.

'I have had the children's photographs taken,' he explained. 'Show yours to Mma Ramotswe, Motholeli.'

The girl pushed her wheelchair forward and gave her photograph to Mma Ramotswe.

'That is a very nice photograph to have,' she said. 'Is Mr JLB Matekoni taking you back now, or are you going to eat in town?'

'We have been shopping,' Mr JLB Matekoni said quickly. 'We may have one or two more things to do.'

'We will go back to his house soon,' the girl said. 'We are living with Mr JLB Matekoni now.'

Mr JLB Matekoni felt his heart jump. 'I am going to have a heart attack and die now,' he thought.

Mma Ramotswe looked at Mr JLB Matekoni.

'They are staying at your house?' she said. 'This is something new. Have they just come?'

'Yesterday,' he said slowly.

Mma Ramotswe looked down at the children and then at Mr JLB Matekoni.

'I think we should have a talk,' she said. 'You children stay here for a moment. Mr JLB Matekoni and I are going to the post office.'

He followed her into the post office with his head down, like a schoolboy who had been caught doing something wrong. She would not marry him now. He had lost her because he had been dishonest and stupid. And it was all Mma Potokwane's fault!

Mma Ramotswe put down her basket of letters.

'Why did you not tell me about these children?' she asked.

He could not look at her. 'I was going to tell you,' he said. 'I was at the orphan farm yesterday. The water pump was broken. It's very old and it will have to be changed soon ...'

'Yes, yes,' said Mma Ramotswe. 'But what about these children?'

'Mma Potokwane is a very strong woman,' he said. 'She told me I should take some foster children. I did not want to do it before I talked to you, but she did not listen to me. She brought the children to meet me. I had no choice.'

'So,' she said, 'you agreed to take these children. And now they think they are going to stay.'

'Yes, I suppose that is true,' he said quietly.

'And for how long?'

Mr JLB Matekoni took a deep breath. 'For as long as they need a home. That is what I offered them.'

To his surprise, Mr JLB Matekoni began to feel more confident. He had done nothing wrong. He had not stolen anything or killed anyone. He had just offered to change the lives of two poor children. If Mma Ramotswe did not like that, there was nothing he could do about it now.

Mma Ramotswe suddenly laughed. 'Well, Mr JLB Matekoni,' she said. 'Nobody can say you are not a kind man. You are, I think, the kindest man in Botswana. I do not know anybody else who would do that.'

Mr JLB Matekoni stared at her. 'You are not cross?'

'I was,' she said. 'But only for a short time. One minute maybe. But then I thought, "Do I want to marry the kindest man in Botswana? I do. Can I be a mother to these children? I can." That is what I thought, Mr JLB Matekoni.'

He looked at her, not believing what he had heard. 'You are a very kind woman yourself, Mma.'

'We must not stand here and talk about kindness,' she said. 'There are two children there. Let's take them back to Zebra Drive and show them where they are going to live. Then this afternoon I can collect them from your house and bring them to my home. My home is more …'

She stopped herself, but he did not mind.

'I know your house is more comfortable than mine,' he said. 'And it would be better for them if you looked after them.'

They walked back to the children together.

'I'm going to marry this lady,' said Mr JLB Matekoni. 'She will be your mother soon.'

The boy looked surprised, but the girl lowered her eyes politely.

'Thank you, Mma,' she said, 'We shall try to be good children.'

'That is good,' said Mma Ramotswe. 'We shall be a very happy family. I know it already.'

Mma Ramotswe and the boy drove off in her little white van. Mr JLB Matekoni took the girl in his pick-up. When he got to Zebra Drive, Mma Ramotswe and Puso were waiting for them. The boy was excited and ran to greet his sister.

'This is a very good house,' he shouted. 'Look, there are trees and fruit. I will have a room at the back.'

Mr JLB Matekoni let Mma Ramotswe show the children around the house. Her father, Obed Ramotswe, had done a very fine job, he thought. He had given Botswana one of its finest ladies.

While Mma Ramotswe was making lunch for the children, Mr JLB Matekoni telephoned the garage. The younger assistant answered. His voice was high and excited.

'I am glad that you telephoned, Rra,' he said. 'The police came. They wanted to speak to you about your maid. She had a gun in her bag and they have arrested her.'

That was all the assistant knew, and so Mr JLB Matekoni put down the telephone. His maid had had a gun! He knew she was lazy and dishonest, but this? Was she going to kill someone?

He went into the kitchen.

'My maid has been arrested by the police,' he told Mma Ramotswe. 'She had a gun in her bag.'

Mma Ramotswe put down her spoon. 'I am not surprised,' she said. 'That woman was very dishonest.'

Mr JLB Matekoni and Mma Ramotswe decided to spend the rest of the day with the children. Mr JLB Matekoni telephoned his assistants and told them to close the garage until the next morning.

'I told them to use the time to study,' he said to Mma Ramotswe. 'But they won't study. They will go and chase girls. There is nothing in those young men's heads.'

'Many young people are like that,' said Mma Ramotswe. 'They think only of dances and clothes and loud music. We were like that too, remember?'

Mma Ramotswe called the No. 1 Ladies' Detective Agency. Mma Makutsi answered and said that she had completed her report on the Badule matter. They would have to talk about that, Mma Ramotswe told her.

Lunch was ready, though. It was time to sit down to eat as a family for the first time.

'We are grateful for this food,' said Mma Ramotswe. 'There are brothers and sisters who do not have good food on their table. We think of them and wish them food in the future. And we thank the Lord, who has brought these children into our lives so we can all be happy and the children can have a home with us. And we think of the mother and father of these children, who are watching us from above.'

Mr JLB Matekoni's heart was so full of emotion that he could say nothing. So he was silent.

Chapter 11   Oswald Ranta

'I have read your report,' said Mma Ramotswe, when Mma Makutsi arrived for work the next morning. 'It is complete and well written.'

'Thank you, Mma,' said Mma Makutsi. 'I am happy that my first case was not a difficult one. I mean, it was not difficult to find out what we needed to know. But those questions at the end of my report – they are difficult. I don't know how to solve them.'

'Yes,' said Mma Ramotswe, looking at the report. 'They are difficult for me too. I am older than you, but I do not have the answer to every problem that comes along.'

'But what can we do?' said Mma Makutsi. 'If we tell Mr Badule about this man, he may make trouble. Then the boy might not get money for school. That would not be good for the boy.'

'I know,' said Mma Ramotswe. 'But we cannot lie to Mr Badule. A detective must not lie to a client.'

'Yes, but should we tell him everything? We could say, "You are right, your wife is seeing another man," and stop there. We are not lying, are we? We are just not telling all the truth.'

In this case, thought Mma Ramotswe, the most important thing was what happened to the boy. He should not suffer just because his mother had behaved badly. But was anyone really unhappy in this situation? The well-dressed wife was happy because she had a rich man to buy her clothes. The rich man was happy because he had a stylish lady friend. The religious wife was happy because she could live in her village and her husband came home every weekend. The boy was happy because he was going to an expensive school.

'It's Mr Badule,' said Mma Ramotswe. 'We have to make him happy. We have to tell him what is happening, but we must make him accept it. If he accepts it, then the whole problem goes away.'

Mma Makutsi was not sure that this was possible. But she was happy that Mma Ramotswe had made a decision, and she would not have to tell any lies.

But there were other cases too. Mrs Curtin had sent a letter, asking Mma Ramotswe if she had found anything out about her son. 'I have the feeling,' she wrote, 'that you will discover something for me.'

Mma Ramotswe knew that the young man had died on the commune. Someone had harmed the boy, and now she had to find someone who could do harm: Mr Oswald Ranta.

♦

The little white van entered the university car park. Mma Ramotswe got out and looked around. She passed the university every day but she had never been inside. She had not gone to university. But here there were teachers and doctors, people who had written books, people whose heads contained more knowledge than the heads of most people.

She found a map of the university on a wall. The Department of Mathematics was here. The Department of Engineering was over there. And there, something called Information.

She went looking for Information and came to a small building near the African Languages department. Mma Ramotswe knocked on the door and went inside.

A thin woman was sitting behind a desk. She looked bored.

'I am looking for Mr Ranta,' said Mma Ramotswe. 'I believe he works here.'

'*Dr* Ranta,' said the woman. 'He is not just Mr Ranta. He is *Dr* Ranta.'

'I am sorry,' said Mma Ramotswe. 'Where is he, please?'

'He is here one moment and then he is gone. That's Dr Ranta.

49

But you could try his office. He has an office here. But most of the time he spends in the bedroom.'

'Oh,' said Mma Ramotswe. 'He is a ladies' man, this Dr Ranta?'

'You could say that,' said the woman. 'And one day the university will catch him. But until then, nobody dares complain.'

So often, thought Mma Ramotswe, other people did your work for you, as this woman was now doing.

'Why do people not complain?' she asked.

'The girls are afraid to speak,' said the woman. 'And the other teachers all have secrets too. There are a lot of people like Dr Ranta here. I can say this because I'm leaving tomorrow. I have found a better job.'

Then the woman told her how to find Dr Ranta's office. As she was leaving, Mma Ramotswe had an idea.

'Perhaps, Mma, Dr Ranta has done nothing wrong,' she said.

She saw immediately that it was going to work. The woman had suffered because of Dr Ranta.

'Oh, yes, he has,' she said angrily. 'He showed an examination paper to a student if she would do what he wanted. I know because the student was my cousin's daughter.'

'But can you prove this?' asked Mma Ramotswe.

'No,' she said. 'He would lie and then nothing would happen.'

'And this girl, Margaret, what did she do?'

'Margaret? Who is Margaret?'

'Your cousin's daughter,' said Mma Ramotswe.

'She is not called Margaret,' said the woman. 'She is called Angel. She did nothing, and he was never caught. Men never get caught, do they?'

'Sometimes they do,' Mma Ramotswe thought. But she only

said goodbye and went to look for Dr Ranta's office.

The door was slightly open. Mma Ramotswe listened and heard the sound of someone typing on a computer keyboard. Dr Ranta was in.

He looked up quickly as she knocked on the door and opened it more.

'Yes, Mma,' he said. 'What do you want?'

'I would like to speak to you, Rra. Have you got a moment?'

He looked at his watch.

'Yes,' he said politely. 'But I haven't got a lot of time. Are you a student?'

Mma Ramotswe sat down. 'No, I am not. I have not been to university. I was busy working for my cousin's husband's company.'

'It is never too late, Mma,' he said. 'We have some very old students here. Of course, you are not very old, but I mean that anybody can study.'

'Maybe,' she said. 'Maybe one day.'

'You can study many things here.'

'Can someone study to be a detective?'

He looked surprised. 'Detective? You can't study that at a university.'

'But I have read that you can, at universities in America.'

'Oh, yes, at American universities you can study anything. Swimming, if you like. But not at the good universities. I studied at Duke, a very good American university.'

He paused. 'He wants me to admire him,' thought Mma Ramotswe. 'That is why he needs all the girls – he needs people to admire him.'

'I would like to spend more time talking with you, Mma,' he said, smiling. 'But I am busy, so I must ask you what this is about.'

'I am sorry to take your time, Rra,' she said. 'I am sure you are very busy. I am just a lady detective …'

He stopped smiling. 'You are a detective?' His voice was colder now.

'It is only a small agency. The No. 1 Ladies' Detective Agency. It is over by Kale Hill. Perhaps you have seen it.'

'I do not go over there,' he said, looking nervous. 'Why do you want to talk to me? Has someone told you to come and speak to me?'

'No. I have come to ask you about something that happened a long time ago. Ten years ago.'

He stared at her. She thought she could smell fear on him.

'Ten years is a long time. People do not remember.'

'No,' she agreed. 'They forget. But some things are difficult to forget. For example, a mother will not forget her son.'

As she spoke, he changed again. He got up from his chair and laughed.

'Oh,' he said. 'I see now. It's that American woman, the one who always asks questions. She is paying you to dig up the past again. Will she never stop? Will she never learn?'

'Learn what?' asked Mma Ramotswe.

He was standing at the window, looking at the students on the path below.

'Learn that there is nothing to learn,' he said. 'That boy is dead. Probably lost in the Kalahari. He went for a walk and never came back. It's easy to get lost in the desert, you know. All the trees look the same and there are no hills to guide you, so you get lost. Especially if you are a white man in a foreign land.'

'But I don't believe that he got lost and died,' said Mma Ramotswe. 'I believe something else happened to him.'

He turned to look at her.

'For example?' he said angrily.

'I am not sure,' she said. 'How could I know? I wasn't there.' She paused, and then added quietly, 'But you were.'

She could hear his breathing as he returned to his chair. From the window, she could hear the students outside laughing and shouting.

'You say I was there,' he said, staring at her. 'What do you mean?'

She stared back. 'I mean that you were living there. You saw him every day. You saw him on the day that he died. I'm sure you know something.'

'I told the police, and I have told the Americans who came asking questions. I saw him that morning, once, and I saw him at lunch. I told them what we had for lunch. I described the clothes he was wearing. I told them everything.'

He was lying, thought Mma Ramotswe. It was easy to see. How could other people not know he was lying?

'I do not believe you, Rra,' she said. 'You are lying to me.'

He opened his mouth slightly, then closed it.

'Our talk has ended, Mma,' he said. 'I am sorry I cannot help you.'

'Very well, Rra,' said Mma Ramotswe. 'But you could help that poor American woman. She is a mother. You had a mother. But I know that you do not care. And not just because she is a white woman from America. If she was a woman from your own village, you wouldn't care about her, would you?'

He smiled at her. 'We have finished our talk.'

'But people can sometimes be made to care,' she said.

'In a minute, I am going to telephone the university police. I think I will say that you were trying to steal something. They would come quickly. It might be difficult for you, Mma.'

'I wouldn't do that if I were you, Rra,' she said. 'You see, I know all about Angel.'

Her words had an immediate effect. He sat up straight in

53

his chair and she could smell the fear again. This time it was stronger.

'Yes,' she said. 'I know about Angel and the examination paper. I have a letter that describes everything that happened. It is back in my office right now. What are you going to do, Rra? What will you do in Gaborone if you lose your university job? Will you go back to your village? Help with the cows again?'

Blackmail, she thought. That was what she was doing, blackmail. And this is what a blackmailer feels. The feeling of complete power over another person.

'You cannot do that … I will say I didn't do it … You cannot prove anything …'

'But I *can* prove it,' she said. 'There is Angel, and there is another girl, who will lie and say that you gave her examination questions too. She is cross with you and she will lie. There will be two girls with the same story.'

His lips were dry, she noticed. He moved his tongue over them. His shirt was wet under the arms.

'I do not like doing this, Rra,' she said. 'But this is my job. Sometimes I have to do things like this. There is a very sad American woman who only wants to say goodbye to her son. You don't care about her, but I do. I think her feelings are more important than yours.

'So I am going to offer you something. You tell me what happened. If you do, I promise you that Angel and her friend will say nothing.'

His breathing was strange, now – short, quick breaths.

'I did not kill him,' he said. 'I did not kill him.'

'Now you are speaking the truth,' said Mma Ramotswe. 'But you must tell me what happened, and where his body is. That is what I want to know.'

'Are you going to the police?' he asked.

'No, this story is just for his mother. That is all.'

He closed his eyes. 'I cannot talk here. You can come to my house.'

'I will come this evening.'

'No,' he said. 'Tomorrow evening.'

'I shall come this evening,' she said. 'That woman has waited for ten years. She must not wait any longer.'

'All right. I shall write down the address. You can come tonight at nine o'clock.'

'I shall come at eight,' said Mma Ramotswe. 'Not every woman will do what you tell her to do.'

She felt her heart jumping as she walked back to the little white van. She did not know where she had found the strength, but it had been there, deep inside her.

Chapter 12   At Tlokweng Road Speedy Motors

While Mma Ramotswe was blackmailing Dr Oswald Ranta – for good reasons, of course – Mr JLB Matekoni took his two foster children to the garage for the afternoon.

The girl, Motholeli, wanted to see him work, and he had agreed. A garage was not a good place for children, with all those heavy tools and machines. But he could ask one of the assistants to look after them while he was working. A visit to the garage might make the boy more interested in mechanical work.

He parked in front of his office door and the boy ran off immediately. Mr JLB Matekoni had to call him back.

'This place is dangerous,' he warned. 'You must stay with one of the boys over there.'

He called over the younger assistant. 'Stop what you are doing and watch these two while I am working. Make sure they don't get hurt.'

The assistant smiled at the children. He seemed happy with

his new job. 'He's the lazy one,' thought Mr JLB Matekoni.

The garage was busy. A football team's bus needed work. With the help of the other assistant, Mr JLB Matekoni took the engine out of the bus. Motholeli watched them carefully from her wheelchair. Her brother looked once, and then looked away. He began to draw pictures in a pool of oil on the ground.

When Mr JLB Matekoni paused in his work, Motholeli asked, 'What is happening now, Rra? Are you going to change those rings? Are they important?'

Mr JLB Matekoni looked at the boy. 'Do you see what I am doing, Puso?'

The boy smiled weakly.

'He is drawing a picture of a house in the oil,' said the younger assistant.

'May I come closer?' asked the girl. 'I will not get in the way.'

Mr JLB Matekoni agreed, and she pushed her wheelchair closer. He showed her the part of the engine that he was working on.

'You hold this for me,' he said, and she held the tool he gave her.

'Good. Now turn it. Not too much. Good.'

He put the tool back in the toolbox and looked at her. Her eyes were bright with interest. He could see that she loved engines. His younger assistant did not, and that was why he would never be a good mechanic. But this girl, this strange, serious girl, could become a good mechanic. He had never seen a girl become a mechanic, but why not? People thought detectives were always men, but look at Mma Ramotswe.

Motholeli looked at him politely.

'You are not cross with me, Rra?' she said. 'I am not annoying you?'

He put his hand gently on her arm.

'Of course I am not cross,' he said. 'I am proud. I am proud that I have a daughter who will be a great mechanic. Is that what you want?'

'Yes, I have always loved engines,' she said. 'But I have never had the chance to do anything.'

'That will change now,' said Mr JLB Matekoni. 'You can come with me on Saturday mornings and help me here. Would you like that? We can make a special work place for you – a low one, so you can sit in your chair and work.'

'You are very kind, Rra,' she said.

When they had finally put the engine back, Motholeli smiled. 'That bus is happy now,' she said.

Mr JLB Matekoni looked at her proudly. He was no longer worried about the future of Tlokweng Road Speedy Motors.

Chapter 13   Michael Curtin

Mma Ramotswe felt afraid. She had been afraid only once or twice before in her work as Botswana's only lady detective. (Mma Makutsi, she thought, was only an *assistant* detective.)

Of course, there was no real reason to be afraid to go to Dr Ranta's house. There would be neighbours next door, there would be the lights of cars in the road. Dr Ranta was a ladies' man, not a murderer.

But sometimes very ordinary people can be murderers. She had read that most people knew the person who murdered them. Mothers killed their children. Husbands killed their wives. Wives killed their husbands. Employees killed their employers. Perhaps murder happened in exactly this situation – a quiet talk in a small house, while people did ordinary things just a short distance away.

Mr JLB Matekoni knew that something was wrong with

Mma Ramotswe. He had come to dinner to tell her about his visit to his maid, who was now in prison. He decided to tell his story first, to take her mind off her problem, whatever it was.

'I have asked a lawyer to see Florence,' he said.

Mma Ramotswe put a large serving of beans on Mr JLB Matekoni's plate.

'Did she explain anything?' she asked.

'She was shouting when I first arrived,' he said. 'The guards said: "Please control your wife and tell her to shut her big mouth." I had to tell them twice that she was not my wife.'

'But why was she shouting?' asked Mma Ramotswe. 'She is a silly woman, but I'm sure she knows that shouting won't help her.'

'She knows that, I think,' said Mr JLB Matekoni. 'She was shouting because she was so cross. She said something else too. She said your name. I don't know why.'

'And the gun? Did she explain the gun?'

'She said the gun did not belong to her. She said that it belonged to a boyfriend and that he was coming to collect it. Then she said that she didn't know it was in her bag. She thought it was a package of meat.'

'Nobody will believe that,' said Mma Ramotswe.

'That's what the lawyer said to me on the telephone,' said Mr JLB Matekoni. 'The courts don't believe people who say they did not know they had a gun. They send them to prison for at least a year.'

Mr JLB Matekoni looked at Mma Ramotswe. She was nervous about something. In a marriage, it would be important not to have secrets. Of course, he had kept his two foster children a secret from Mma Ramotswe. But now they should have no secrets.

'Mma Ramotswe,' he said, 'you are thinking about something. Is something wrong? Is it something I have said?'

She looked at her watch.

'It's not about you,' she said. 'I have to speak to somebody tonight. It's about Mma Curtin's son. I am worried about this person that I have to see.'

She told him about Dr Ranta. She said that she did not think he would murder her, but she could not be sure.

He listened quietly. When she had finished, he said, 'You cannot go. I cannot let my future wife do something dangerous like that.'

She looked at him. 'It makes me very pleased to know that you are worried about me. But I am a detective. This is my job.'

Mr JLB Matekoni looked unhappy. 'If you go, then I shall go too. I shall wait outside. He need not know I am there.'

'All right,' she said. 'We will take my van. You can wait outside while I am talking to him.'

'And if there is a problem, you can shout,' he said.

They finished the meal, both of them feeling better. Mr JLB Matekoni took the plates to the kitchen, and Mma Ramotswe went to look at the children. Motholeli had been reading to her brother in his bedroom. Now Puso was almost asleep and the girl was sleepy herself.

'It is time for you to go to bed too,' she said to the girl. 'Mr JLB Matekoni says you have had a busy day fixing engines.'

She pushed Motholeli back to her own room and the girl got into bed.

'Are you happy here, Motholeli?' she asked.

'I am so happy,' said the girl. 'And every day my life is getting happier.'

♦

They were parked outside Dr Ranta's house.

'I will be ready,' said Mr JLB Matekoni. 'If you shout, I will hear you.'

They looked at the house. It was an ordinary house with an untidy garden. Dr Ranta clearly did not employ a gardener, thought Mma Ramotswe. This was wrong. A person with a good job, like Dr Ranta, should employ people at home. There were so many people who needed work.

'He is selfish,' said Mma Ramotswe.

'That's exactly what I was thinking,' said Mr JLB Matekoni.

She opened the door of the van and got out. Mr JLB Matekoni watched her walk to the front door and knock. Dr Ranta had been waiting. He quickly opened the door and she went inside.

'Is your friend in the van coming in, Mma?' said Dr Ranta.

'No,' she said. 'He will wait for me outside.'

Dr Ranta laughed. 'So you will feel safe?'

She did not answer his question. 'You have a nice house,' she said. 'You are fortunate.'

He led her into the living room and they sat down.

'I don't want to waste time talking to you,' he said. 'I will speak only because you are making trouble for me and because someone is lying about me.'

He was hurt, thought Mma Ramotswe. He had been beaten – and by a woman. That would be very embarrassing for a man like him.

'How did Michael Curtin die?' she asked.

'I worked there,' he began. 'I was studying what they were doing, for the university. But I knew their commune would fail. I knew it would not work.

'I lived in the big house. The boss was a German, Burkhardt Fischer. He had a wife, Marcia. There was also a South African woman, Carla Smit. And the American boy.

'We were all friends, except that Burkhardt did not like me. He tried to make me leave but he couldn't. I was working for the university. He told lies about me, but they didn't believe him.

'The American boy was very polite. He could speak some Setswana and people liked him. The South African woman liked him too. Soon they were sharing the same room. She did everything for him. She cooked his food, cleaned his clothes. Then she became interested in me. I didn't make her do it, but she was with me at the same time that she was with that boy. She said she wanted to tell him, but she didn't want to hurt him. So we saw each other secretly.

'Burkhardt guessed what was happening. He called me into his office and said he would tell the American boy if I didn't stop seeing Carla. He became angry and said he would complain about me to the university. So I told him I would stop seeing Carla.

'But I did not. Why should I? We met each other in the evenings. She told the boy that she liked walking in the bush at night. He didn't because he thought it was dangerous. So he did not go with her.

'We had a place where we went to be alone together. It was a small hut in the fields. That night we were in the hut together. There was a full moon outside. I heard someone outside and I opened the door very slowly. The American boy was outside.

'He said, "What are you doing here?" I said nothing, and then he saw Carla. Of course, then he knew what was happening.

'At first he didn't say anything. Then he began to run – not back to the big house, but into the bush.

'Carla shouted for me to go after him, so I did. He ran fast. I caught him once but he got away. I followed him through the bush, and cut myself on the arms and legs. It was very dangerous.

'I caught him again, but he pulled away from me. We were on the edge of a deep ditch. He fell into the ditch. I looked down and saw him lying on the ground. He was not moving.

'I climbed down and looked at him. He had broken his neck

when he fell, and he was not breathing.

'I ran back to Carla and told her what had happened. She came back with me to the ditch. He was clearly dead and she started to scream.

'When she had stopped screaming, we talked about what to do. I said that if we reported what had happened, nobody would believe that it was an accident. People would say that we had had a fight about Carla, and that I killed him. I knew Burkhardt would say bad things about me to the police.

'So we decided to bury the body and say that we knew nothing about it. There were some anthills near us, so I hid the body inside one and covered it with leaves and stones. I did a good job, because the game tracker never found it.

'The police asked us questions and we both said nothing. She became very quiet and did not want to see me anymore. After some time, she left. She told me that she was going to have a child – his child, not mine. I left too, one month later.

'I went to study at Duke University. She did not go back to South Africa. I heard that she went to Bulawayo in Zimbabwe, and that she found a job running a hotel there. I think she is still there.'

He stopped and looked at Mma Ramotswe. 'That is the truth, Mma,' he said. 'I did not kill him. I have told you the truth.'

'I know,' said Mma Ramotswe. She paused. 'I am not going to tell the police. I promised you that I would not. But I am going to tell the mother what happened. I will ask her to make the same promise – not to go to the police.'

'And those girls?' asked Dr Ranta. 'They won't make trouble for me?'

'No,' said Mma Ramotswe. 'There will be no trouble.'

'But what about the letter?' he asked. 'The one from the other girl?'

Mma Ramotswe got up and opened the front door. Mr JLB

He had broken his neck when he fell, and he was not breathing.

Matekoni was sitting in the van. He looked up when she opened the door. She walked out of the house.

'Well, Dr Ranta,' she said quietly. 'I think you are a man who has lied to a lot of people. Especially to women. Now something new has happened to you. A woman has lied to you and you have believed her. There was no girl.'

She walked to the van. Dr Ranta stood at the door watching her. She knew he would not hurt her. Actually, if he had a conscience, he should be grateful to her. Now, finally, the events of ten years ago could rest in peace. But she doubted that he had much of a conscience.

Chapter 14   Bulawayo

She left early, when the sky was still dark. She drove the little white van along the Francistown Road. Just before she passed the road to Mochudi, the sun came up. For a few minutes, the whole world was gold – the tree, the grass, the dust. The sun was a great red ball in the sky. It went up slowly over Africa. As it did, the natural colours of the world returned.

Mma Ramotswe liked the drive to Francistown, although today she was going further, over the border and into Zimbabwe. Mr JLB Matekoni had not wanted her to go.

'It is more dangerous than Botswana,' he had said. 'What will happen if your van breaks down?'

She did not like him to worry, but it was important to make it clear: she would make the decisions in these matters. You could not let the husband make decisions for the No. 1 Ladies' Detective Agency. It was not called the No. 1 Ladies' (and Husband's) Detective Agency. Mr JLB Matekoni was a good mechanic, but he was not a detective.

So she was driving to Bulawayo. By nine o'clock, she was

passing through Mahalapye, where her father, Obed Ramotswe, had been born. If the little white van broke down, she could knock on any door and expect to receive help.

She stopped at Francistown and drank a cup of tea at a hotel. Then she crossed the border and drove into Bulawayo, a town of wide streets and leafy trees. She would stay with a friend here.

♦

It was easy to find the South African woman. Mma Ramotswe's friend made some telephone calls and got the name and address of the hotel. It was an old but well-kept building and there was a noisy bar somewhere inside. There was a sign with the name of the hotel manager: *Carla Smit*. This was the end of the search.

'I am Carla. And you are …?'

Mma Ramotswe looked at the woman sitting behind an untidy desk. 'She thinks I have come for a job,' she thought.

'My name is Precious Ramotswe,' she said. 'I'm from Gaborone. And I have not come to ask for a job.'

The woman smiled. 'So many people do,' she said. 'There is such terrible unemployment.'

'We are lucky down there in Botswana,' said Mma Ramotswe. 'We do not have these troubles.'

'I know,' said Carla. 'I lived there for a couple of years. It was a long time ago. But I hear that things haven't changed much in Botswana. That's why you are lucky.'

'You preferred the old Africa?'

Carla answered carefully. 'I was a South African, but I did not like apartheid. I left South Africa to get away from it. Not all white people liked apartheid, you know.'

Mma Ramotswe had not wanted to embarrass her. 'I didn't mean that,' she said. 'I meant the old Africa, where there were fewer people without jobs. People had a place then. They belonged to their village, to their family. They had their lands.'

Carla relaxed. 'Yes, but we cannot stop the world, can we? Africa has these problems now. We have to try to solve them.'

Mma Ramotswe looked at her hands, and began speaking. 'Ten years ago, you lived out near Molepolole. You were there when an American named Michael Curtin disappeared.'

She stopped. Carla was staring at her with wide eyes.

'I am not the police,' said Mma Ramotswe quickly. 'I have not come here to question you.'

'Then why do you want to talk about that? It happened a long time ago. He disappeared. That's all.'

'No,' said Mma Ramotswe. 'That is not all. I know what happened. You and Oswald Ranta were there, in that hut, when Michael found you. He fell into a ditch and broke his neck. You hid the body because Oswald was afraid that the police would think he killed Michael. That is what happened.'

Carla said nothing, but Mma Ramotswe could see that she was shocked. Dr Ranta had told the truth.

'You did not kill Michael,' she said. 'But you hid the body. Because of that, his mother never knew what had happened to him. That was the wrong thing to do. But you can make things better. And you can do it safely.'

'What can I do?' said Carla quietly.

'You can end his mother's search,' she said. 'She only wants to say goodbye to her son. She just wants to know, that's all.'

'I don't know,' said Carla. 'Oswald would be angry …'

Mma Ramotswe interrupted her. 'Oswald agrees.'

'Then why can't *he* tell her?' said Carla, suddenly angry. 'He did it. I only lied to protect him.'

'Yes,' said Mma Ramotswe. 'It's his fault. But he is not a good man. He cannot say he is sorry. But you can. You can meet this woman and tell her what happened. And you can tell her that you are sorry.'

Carla looked down. 'I don't see why …. It's been such a long time …'

Mma Ramotswe stopped her. 'And you are the mother of her grandchild, aren't you? Mma Curtin has no son now. But there is a …'

'Boy,' said Carla. 'He is called Michael too. He is nine, almost ten.'

Mma Ramotswe smiled. 'You must bring the child to her, Mma,' she said. 'You are a mother. You know what that means.'

Mma Ramotswe got up and walked over to the woman's desk.

'You know you must do this,' she said.

She took the woman's hand and held it gently. It was dark, from sun and heat and hard work.

'Mma Curtin is ready to come to Botswana,' she said. 'She will come in a day or two if I tell her. Can you leave this place, just for a few days?'

'I have an assistant,' said Carla. 'She can run the hotel.'

'And the boy, Michael? Won't he be happy to see his grandmother?'

Carla looked up at her.

'Yes, Mma Ramotswe,' she said. 'You are right.'

♦

Mma Ramotswe returned to Gaborone late the next day. Her maid, Rose, had stayed in the house to look after the children. They were asleep when Mma Ramotswe arrived home. She went to their bedroom and listened to their soft breathing as they slept. Then, tired from the drive, she went to bed.

She was in the office early the next morning. Rose would take care of the children. Mma Makutsi had arrived before her, and was sitting at her desk, typing a report.

'Mr Badule,' she said. 'I am reporting the end of the case.'

'I thought you wanted me to handle that,' said Mma Ramotswe.

'I was not brave enough at first,' said Mma Makutsi. 'But he came in yesterday. You were not here and I had to talk to him.'

'And?' asked Mma Ramotswe.

'And I told him that his wife was seeing another man.'

'What did he say?'

'He was upset. He looked very sad.'

'That's not surprising,' said Mma Ramotswe.

'Yes, but then I told him he should not do anything. I said his wife was not seeing this man for her own pleasure. I said she was doing it for the son. She was seeing a rich man so his son would go to a good school.'

Mma Ramotswe was surprised. 'He believed that?' she said.

'Yes,' said Mma Makutsi. 'He seemed pleased. So now he is happy, his wife is happy, and the boy can stay in the private school. And the wife's lover and the wife's lover's wife are also happy. It is a good result.'

Mma Ramotswe was not so sure. There was something wrong with this solution. She would have to talk about it with Mma Makutsi when they had more time.

♦

Some days passed with no new clients. Mma Makutsi cleaned her typewriter and bought some new tea things. Mma Ramotswe wrote letters to old friends and added up the company's money. There was not a lot, but they were not losing money, and she had been happy and had done interesting things. That was as important as making a lot of money.

Three days later, Andrea Curtin arrived. In the office of the No. 1 Ladies' Detective Agency, Mrs Curtin met her grandson and his mother. While Carla told her what had happened ten years ago, Mma Ramotswe took the boy for a walk.

He was a serious, polite boy, and he seemed interested in stones.

In the office of the No. 1 Ladies' Detective Agency, Mrs Curtin met her grandson and his mother.

As they walked, he stopped to look at or pick up small rocks.

'I want to study geology,' he told Mma Ramotswe. 'There is a geologist who stays in our hotel sometimes. He shows me how to find interesting rocks.'

Mma Ramotswe smiled. 'That's like being a detective,' she said. 'Looking for things.'

When they returned, Carla and Mrs Curtin were sitting together. The older woman looked peaceful and happy. Mma Ramotswe knew that she had found what she was looking for.

They drank tea together quietly. The boy had a gift for his grandmother, a small stone animal which he had made himself. She took it, and kissed him, just like any other grandmother.

Mma Ramotswe also had a gift for the American woman. It was a basket that she had bought on her way back from Bulawayo, from a woman sitting by the road. The woman was poor, and Mma Ramotswe had wanted to help her. It was a traditional Botswana basket, with a traditional picture on its side.

She explained the picture to Mrs Curtin. 'This is a giraffe, and these little marks are the tears of the giraffe. The giraffe gives its tears to the women and they put them in the basket.'

The American woman took the basket politely, with both hands, in the correct Botswana way.

'You are very kind, Mma,' she said. 'But why did the giraffe give its tears?'

Mma Ramotswe was surprised. She had never thought about it. 'I suppose it means that we can all give something,' she said. 'A giraffe has nothing else to give – only its tears.'

Did it really mean that, she wondered. For a moment, she imagined a giraffe looking down from the trees. She thought of the beauty that there was in Africa, and the love.

The boy looked at the basket. 'Is that true, Mma?'

Mma Ramotswe smiled. 'I hope so,' she said.

ACTIVITIES

Chapters 1–2

Before you read

1 Mma Ramotswe is a private detective in Botswana, in Africa. What other famous detectives do you know? Where do they solve crimes?

2 Look at the Word List at the back of the book. Check the meaning of new words. Then answer these questions.
   a Which are words for animals?
   b Which are words for people?
   c Which are words for groups of people working together?

3 Read the Introduction to this book. Then discuss what you have learnt about:
   a Mma Precious Ramotswe
   b Alexander McCall Smith
   c Botswana

4 Look at the map opposite page 1 of this book and find:
   a a desert
   b the capital of Botswana
   c a road that connects a number of towns and cities

While you read

5 Choose the correct descriptions for each of these people.

   Mr JLB Matekoni   Mma Ramotswe   Florence
   Mma Makutsi   Mrs Curtin   Michael   Burkhardt

   a a German who lived on a farm   ....
   b the owner of a car repair business   ....
   c an American who disappeared   ....
   d Mma Ramotswe's secretary   ....
   e Mr JLB Matekoni's maid   ....
   f Botswana's only female private
        detective   ....
   g a woman who wants Mma
        Ramotswe's help   ....

71

After you read

6   Number these in the correct order. Write the numbers 1–8.

    a   Mma Makutsi cleans her typewriter.   .....

    b   Mma Ramotswe agrees to help Mrs Curtin.   .....

    c   Mma Ramotswe meets Florence.   .....

    d   Mr JLB Matekoni decides his maid must go.   .....

    e   Mr JLB Matekoni and Mma Ramotswe have lunch.   .....

    f   Mr JLB Matekoni asks Mma Ramotswe to marry him.   .....

    g   Mr JLB Matekoni telephones Mma Ramotswe.   .....

    h   The American woman tells her story.   .....

7   Discuss these questions.

    a   Why has Mr JLB Matekoni never invited Mma Ramotswe to his house?

    b   Why did Michael decide to stay in Botswana?

    c   Why does Mma Ramotswe call Mrs Curtin 'my sister'?

    d   What happened to Michael, do you think?

    e   What can Mma Ramotswe do to help Mrs Curtin?

Chapters 3–4

Before you read

8   Mr JLB Matekoni regularly visits a farm where orphans live. Why does he go there, do you think? What does he do there?

While you read

9   Are these sentences right (✔) or wrong (✗)?

    a   People take their cars to Speedy Motors to make them run faster.   .....

    b   Mr JLB Matekoni has known Mrs Potokwane for a long time.   .....

    c   The girl in the wheelchair has no relatives.   .....

    d   The girl does not say why she is in the wheelchair.   .....

    e   Mma Ramotswe drives to Silokwolela alone.   .....

    f   Mma Potsane is afraid of the commune at night.   .....

    g   People do not live at the commune any more.   .....

    h   Mma Potsane thinks the American boy ran away.   .....

    i   Mma Potsane knows the people in the photograph.   .....

After you read

10 Put these words in the right sentences.

careless   information   noisy   photograph

polite   pump   ring   sweets   water

a Mr JLB Matekoni thinks his assistants are ....

b Mr JLB gives some .... to the orphan children.

c Mma Potokwane has a broken ....

d The girl in the wheelchair is very ....

e Her wheelchair is .... so Mr JLB Matekoni fixes it.

f The girl gives Mr JLB Matekoni some ....

g Mr JLB Matekoni has given Mma Ramotswe a ....

h Mma Potsane gives Mma Ramotswe some ....

i Mma Ramotswe takes a .... from the farm house.

11 Work with another student. Have this conversation.

Student A: You are Mr JLB Matekoni. Tell your friend about
your problems with your assistants. Then ask
your friend what you should do about them.

Student B: You are Mr JLB Matekoni's friend. Tell him what
you would do about his assistants if you were
him.

Chapters 5–6

Before you read

12 Discuss these questions.

a Read the title of Chapter 5. Who are the children, do you
think? What will you learn from their story?

b Read the title of Chapter 6. What will Mma Makutsi's
promotion be, do you think? How will she feel about it?

While you read

13 Answer these questions.

a Who does Mr JLB Matekoni usually see on
Saturday mornings?   ....

b Who tells him the children's story?   ....

c Who did the bushmen bury?   ....

d Who saved the boy?   ....

73

    e How long did the children stay in
        the hospital? ....

    f Who told the orphan farm about
        the children? ....

14 Who is speaking?

    a 'This is not a chicken farm.' ....

    b 'Men choose the beautiful girls.' ....

    c 'He is dead. But he is there.' ....

    d 'I do not like the way he looks.' ....

    e 'You will be an assistant detective.' ....

After you read

15 Discuss the people below. Put these adjectives in a table like
the one below, and add other words.

uncomfortable   intelligent   cruel   handsome

kind   brave   honest   hard-working   friendly

Mr JLB Matekoni	Mma Makutsi	the girl in the wheelchair	Oswald Ranta

16 Mr JLB Matekoni has agreed to take the children without telling
Mma Ramotswe. Do you think this is a mistake? Why (not)?

17 Work with another student. Have this conversation.

    Student A: You are Mma Makutsi. Tell your friend about your
               promotion. Talk about your feelings. Say what
               you hope you will do.

    Student B: You are Mma Makutsi's friend. Give her some
               advice about her new job.

Chapters 7–8

Before you read

18 Discuss these questions.

    a In Chapter 7, Mma Makutsi gets her first case, about a
        man who thinks his wife is seeing another man. What do
        detectives usually do to solve cases like this?

b In Chapter 8, Mr JLB Matekoni takes the two children to town for the first time. What will they do, do you think?

While you read

19 Which statements are correct? Write *Yes* or *No*.

a Mr Badule is not a very rich man. .....
b His son always did well in school. .....
c Thornhill is a good school. .....
d Mma Makutsi's uncle is not interested in her work. .....
e Mma Makutsi's uncle likes taking notes. .....
f The maids tell Mma Makutsi their employer's name. .....
g Mrs Badule often visits a married man. .....
h Mma Makutsi does not know what to do about the case. .....
i Mr JLB Matekoni wants his foster son to be a mechanic. .....
j The orphan girl thinks that machines are boring. .....
k Mr JLB Matekoni is embarrassed to see Mma Ramotswe. .....

After you read

20 Who is speaking? Who are they talking to? What are they talking about? Discuss these questions.

a '*Aiee!* What have we been doing?'
b 'I do not want to run before I can walk.'
c 'I have not been able to sleep.'
d 'It is like a cloud on wheels.'
e 'There is no shooting in Botswana.'
f 'One day we will have more photographs.'

21 Imagine that you are Mma Ramotswe. You have just seen Mr JLB Matekoni and the two children in the street. Tell another student what is going through your mind.

22 Read Mma Makutsi's report in Chapter 7 again. Then discuss with other students what she should do.

Chapters 9–10

Before you read

23 What do you think? Note down answers to these questions.

 a How does Mr JLB Matekoni's maid, Florence, feel about
   Mr JLB Matekoni's new children?

 b How does she feel about Mma Ramotswe?

 c What will Mma Ramotswe say about the children?

 d Will the children like Mma Ramotswe? Why (not)?

While you read

24 Write the correct word in these sentences.

Mr JLB Matekoni's maid, Florence, asks **(a)**............................. ,
one of her lovers, to help her get a gun. He tells her that people
with illegal guns go to **(b)**............................. . This makes her
happy, because she wants to hurt **(c)**............................. .
Philemon has an extra gun, and he gives it to Florence in a
(d)............................. shopping bag. Another friend,
(e)............................. , has borrowed money from her. She
tells him that he does not need to return the money if he puts
the gun in Mma Ramotswe's **(f)**............................. . He
agrees, but instead he calls the **(g)**............................. .

25 Are these sentences right (✔) or wrong (✗)?

 a The children are too shy to speak to Mma Ramotswe. .....

 b Mma Ramotswe and Mr JLB Matekoni go to the post
   office. .....

 c Mr JLB Matekoni lies about the children. .....

 d Mma Ramotswe is very angry with him. .....

 e The children feel uncomfortable in Mma Ramotswe's
   house. .....

 f The police have caught Mr JLB Matekoni's maid. .....

After you read

26 Work with another student. Have this conversation.

 Student A: You are Paul Monosopati. Explain to your friend
      what Florence asked you to do and what you did.

 Student B: You are a Paul's friend. Ask him why he called
      the police. Tell him what you think about that.

Chapters 11–12

Before you read

27 Discuss these questions.

    a What will Mma Ramotswe say to Mma Makutsi about Mr Badule's case?

    b How will Mma Ramotswe get information from Oswald Ranta?

    c What will happen when Mr JLB Matekoni takes the two children to Speedy Motors?

While you read

28 Circle the correct words.

    a Mma Makutsi does not want to *tell Mr Badule the truth / follow Mma Ramotswe's advice.*

    b Mma Ramotswe tells Oswald Ranta that she is *a detective / a student.*

    c Oswald Ranta is afraid that Mma Ramotswe will talk to *Mrs Curtin / the police.*

    d *The boy / The girl* helps Mr JLB Matekoni work on an engine.

After you read

29 Choose the correct endings to these sentences.

    a Oswald Ranta   likes to draw.

    b The Information woman   enjoys mechanical work.

    c Angel   is a ladies' man.

    d Puso   is afraid to complain.

    e Motholeli   is leaving the job.

30 Discuss these questions.

    a What does Mma Ramotswe think they should do about Mr Badule? Do you agree that this is the best thing to do?

    b Mma Ramotswe thinks she is blackmailing Oswald Ranta. How is she blackmailing him? Is it ever right to use blackmail to get what you want?

Chapters 13–14

Before you read

31 In Chapter 13, Mma Ramotswe finds out what happened to Michael Curtin. Which of these answers is the most likely, do you think? Can you think of other possibilities?

    a Michael was murdered.

    b Michael was killed by an animal.

    c Michael ran away.

32 Chapter 14 is called Bulawayo. Find the city on the map opposite page 1. Where is it?

While you read

33 Complete the story about Michael Curtin. Write one or two words in each space.

Dr Ranta was studying the commune for the **(a)**............... . He was friendly with everyone at the commune except **(b)**............... . The American boy, Michael, began to share a room with **(c)**............... . Then she also became interested in **(d)**............... . One night, Michael found them together inside a **(e)**............... . He ran into the bush and fell into a **(f)**............... . His **(g)**............... was broken and he died. Dr Ranta hid the body in an **(h)**............... . He and Carla said **(i)**............... to the police. Then Carla left and had a **(j)** ....

34 Correct these sentences. Write the correct words.

    a Carla now runs a farm in Bulawayo.   ....

    b At first, Carla first thinks that Mma Ramotswe wants money.   ....

    c Carla thinks that Mma Ramotswe should tell Mrs Curtin about Michael's death.   ....

    d Mma Ramotswe says that Carla's grandson should meet Mrs Curtin.   ....

    e The boy, Michael, gives a gift to Mma Ramotswe.   ....

    f Mma Ramotswe's gift to Mrs Curtin has a picture of a tree on it.   ....

After you read

35 Discuss these questions.

    a Mma Ramotswe thinks there is something wrong with their solution to Mr Badule's problem. Why does she think this?

    b At the end of the story, what more would you like to know about the characters?

Writing

36 You are Motholeli. You have just begun to live at Mma Ramotswe's house. Write a letter to Mma Potokwane and tell her about your new home and your new family.

37 Write a telephone conversation between Carla Smit, in Zimbabwe, and her mother in South Africa, explaining how young Michael met his other grandmother.

38 You are a journalist. Write a report for your newspaper about Florence Peko's arrest. Include interviews with Paul Monosopati and the policeman he called.

39 You are Mr Badule. Mma Makutsi has told you about your wife and your son. You have tried to accept the situation, but something else has happened. Write a letter to Mma Makutsi and tell her about it.

40 You are Mma Ramotswe. Write a reply to Mma Makutsi's report on pages 33 and 34. Give your own ideas about what Mma Makutsi should do.

41 What picture does the book paint of the natural world in Botswana? How important is it to the story?

42 What have you learnt about Botswana and people's lifestyles from this book? Write a list of interesting information.

43 You are a journalist. Write a magazine report about Mma Ramotswe and the No.1 Ladies' Detective Agency. Include information that she has given you.

44 Which is your favourite character in this book? Which one is your least favourite? Why? Write about them.

45 Explain why you think that people around the world enjoy reading McCall Smith's stories about Mma Ramotswe and her friends.

WORD LIST

agency (n) a business that sells a service to people or organisations

ant (n) a very small insect that lives in a large group. Ants live under piles of dirt called **anthills**.

apartheid (n) the old way of life in South Africa, when white people and black people had to live and study separately

arrest (n/v) the act of taking someone away to a police station because they have done something illegal

blackmail (n/v) the act of trying to make someone do something for you by saying that you will tell other people their secrets

bury (v) to put something under the ground and cover it with earth

bush (n) in Africa, wild country that has not been cleared for farming

carbolic soap (n) a strong type of soap

case (n) an event, or a number of events, that police or detectives are trying to learn more about; a situation that exists

charity (n) an organisation that gives money or help to people who need it

client (n) someone who pays for your help

commune (n) a group of people who live together and share the work and the things that they own

conscience (n) the part of your mind that tells you if something is right or wrong

ditch (n) a long narrow hole, often at the side of a road or a field

embassy (n) a group of officials who work for their government in a foreign country, or the building where these people work

engaged (adj) going to be married

foster child (n) a child who has been taken into someone else's family for some time, but is not legally their child

game (n) wild animals that people hunt for food or sport. A **game tracker** helps hunters find game.

geology (n) the study of rocks and the way they have changed since the earth began

giraffe (n) a tall African animal with a very long neck that eats leaves from trees